EDITED

BOOKS BY BARRY LYGA

The Astonishing Adventures of Fanboy & Goth Girl
Boy Toy
Hero-Type
Goth Girl Rising
Wolverine: Worst Day Ever
Mangaman (with Colleen Doran)
After the Red Rain (with Peter Facinelli and Robert DeFranco)
The Secret Sea
Bang
The Hive (with Morgan Baden)
Time Will Tell
Edited
Unedited

THE ARCHVILLAIN SERIES
Archvillain
The Mad Mask
Yesterday Again

THE I HUNT KILLERS TRILOGY
I Hunt Killers
Game
Blood of My Blood

THE FLASH SERIES
Hocus Pocus
Johnny Quick
The Tornado Twins
Crossover Crisis: Green Arrow's Perfect Shot
Crossover Crisis: Supergirl's Sacrifice
Crossover Crisis: The Legends of Forever

EDITED

BARRY LYGA

**BLACK
STONE**
PUBLISHING

Copyright © 2022 by Barry Lyga, LLC
Published in 2022 by Blackstone Publishing
Illustrations © 2011 by Colleen Doran from *Mangaman*,
a graphic novel, by Barry Lyga and Colleen Doran.
Used by permission of Colleen Doran.
Cover design by Sarah Riedlinger
Book design by Blackstone Publishing

The characters and events in this book are fictitious.
Any similarity to real persons, living or dead, is coincidental
and not intended by the author.

Printed in the United States of America

First edition: 2022
ISBN 979-8-200-83240-8
Young Adult Fiction / General

Version 1

CIP data for this book is available
from the Library of Congress

Blackstone Publishing
31 Mistletoe Rd.
Ashland, OR 97520

www.BlackstonePublishing.com

This is a story about Mike.

And it's also a story about Mike and Phil.

Mike loves Phil. *Always.*

Phil loves Mike. *Sometimes.*

Have you ever been in love?

And then did you ever think . . . *Am I really in love? Or is this just an infatuation and am I going to regret sticking around?*

Have you ever thought someone's love would last forever, only to discover that it's less like a water *faucet* and more like a water *balloon*?

That's what happened to Mike, as you'll see.

****

I've written a lot of stories. Google "Barry Lyga" and you'll see them, and if it's on Google, it must be true, right? But I've never really written what you might call, for lack of a better term, a love story.

I've always been interested in stories about young romance, mainly because they never—ever—bear any resemblance to anything I actually experienced when I was young myself. (A million years ago, when diamonds were still coal, children.) And my own high school romance had a not-so-great finale, if you want to know the truth. So I never could wrap my head around high school sweethearts and their happily-ever-afters. And when I started writing my own books, I inevitably disappointed readers who wanted a kiss at the end. I left that to the readers' imaginations. I wasn't cut out for love stories.

And then one day a love story occurred to me. A big one. I mean, cataclysmically huge. The story of Mike and the story of Phil, and the story of Mike and Phil.

****

After doing something stupid that drove away the love of his life, Mike Grayson began to notice that the world itself seemed to be suffering the aftereffects of his bad decision. Reality as he knew it . . . changed . . . and before he could fully understand the ramifications, he found himself on an odyssey unlike any other, trying to figure out how to repair the universe and return his lost Philomel to his side.

It wasn't time travel. It wasn't dimension hopping. It was something deeper and more fundamental, as simple and as complex as ink on paper.

And much to his surprise, this wasn't even the whole story. In fact, there might not even *be* a whole story. It's possible that the missing pieces of Mike's life may end up being the most important part of his world, and the solution to fixing not only his love life, but the entire universe.

****

That, I figured, was worthy of being my first love story.

The story you're about to read is actually a partial version or an iteration, pieces of a larger whole, stitched together to cover the surgical trauma. You can read it on its own or as the companion to a grander, more epic work—and I've provided you the tools to do so, embedded in the text itself. You'll see what I mean. Very soon.

Either way, you will come to live the life of Mike Grayson and understand his story. And my getting there as his creator.

Now turn the page. The world is about to change.

Barry Lyga

At my desk November 17, 2016

(at the beginning of the end

of the world)

HELLO, PHIL

In the beginning, there was light. And then God said, "Let there be darkness." And I said to him, "But it's been there all along, don't you see?"

PROLOGUE:

THE MOMENT I REALIZED I COULD EDIT REALITY.

I was in the auditorium, at the dance, staring at Phil—at her dress, her teal dress, the dress teal and very definitely *not* red.

Phil stared back at me. Her eyes were narrowed to slits, as though against sunlight—even though it was twilight dark, the lights low in that prom-esque way. We were not, of course, attending a prom. This was a charity event. But the light was prom-esque in any event.

"What's wrong with you?" she asked.

"Your dress . . ."

"I didn't wear it for you. I know it's your favorite, but that's not why I—"

"No," I said. "That's not what . . ." Could no one tell? Did no one notice? I turned to George. "George. What was I just saying when she came in? About her dress?"

George blinked. "Uh, you said . . . uh . . . You said, 'I'm glad she wore the teal. That's the best one for her hair color—'"

"This is for charity," Phil interrupted. She was avoiding my eyes now. Her voice was tense. "Maybe it's best if we don't talk or hang out while we're both here."

And then *he* came in. *He* had the good grace to pause at the door before approaching us. *His* face was a melting pot of anger, shock, and some distant relative of resignation.

"Is there a problem?" *he* asked.

George stepped between us, a faithful wall of sanity.

"Dude, I don't think there's a problem," George said.

Then George puffed out his chest, a truly hilarious sight to those who knew him only by sight. But of course, to those who knew the Legend of George (nearly everyone in the auditorium, including *him*) the chest puffery was anything but hilarious. I truly believe *he* would have punched George in the face, given the testosterone and rage in *his* eyes . . . if not for Phil.

"For charity," she insisted, now interposing herself between George and *him*, so that we formed a strange sort of set of interlocking aggressions: George between *him* and me, also between Phil and me, Phil between George and *him*, me still staring at Phil's teal dress (teal!). "This isn't going to turn into some bullshit macho thing. Jesus, Mike. Do you think getting into a fight is going to win me back?"

A fight was, indeed, a possibility I'd considered. I'd never been in a fight. But I could evoke a universe in which I viciously battered *him* into submission. I would win back Phil like a prizefighter wins a belt, not caring—in the throes of that fancy—that by doing so I reduced her to an object. No, in the throes of that fancy I would care only about having her back.

"No one's going to fight," I said.

And in saying it I became convinced it was not only true, but would remain true.

He took Phil's hand, escorting her past George, past me.

I watched them go. Phil did not look over her shoulder, though *he* did, *his* expression now a grotesque mating of still-simmering anger and boiling-over self-satisfaction. I briefly savored the image of my fist in *his* face—repeatedly.

"Dude, I'm proud of you," George said.

I blinked at him. Then I sniffed. "Do you smell chocolate syrup?" I asked. Because *I* smelled chocolate syrup. I also realized, in that moment, that I had actually been smelling it since Phil had entered the auditorium and changed dresses without ever being naked.

George was staring at me now. "Are you all right?"

"No. No. Something is . . ." I could not put "something" into words. It had begun with the strong reek of chocolate syrup upon Phil's entrance—beautiful but somehow wrong in the *red* dress—followed by my wish that she'd instead worn the *teal* dress . . . followed by her not only wearing the teal dress, but also having *always* worn the teal dress.

But . . . no. It had not begun there.

It had begun moments after that, with my realization that I could, in fact, edit reality—when I decided that Phil had, in fact, worn the red dress . . . the one her mother had bought for her to wear not to a prom-esque charity event, *but to the prom itself.*

I hated that dress.

That warm afternoon, one May previous, I caught myself scowling in Phil's full-length mirror. She'd just draped her mom's gift over her body. She caught my scowl, too. After unzipping herself free, her cute little yellow-and-white-patterned sundress shushing to the floor, she smirked, then dipped herself in the flimsy red fabric.

"Zip me," she said, and I stood.

I zipped the red dress, going slowly, one palm pressed to her lower back as though for support. In reality I took (and would take) any opportunity to touch her, any part of her, because every part of her was (and is) sexy. But Phil's sexiness didn't help the dress.

"I don't like it," I confessed.

She posed and twisted and turned and posed again in front of the full-length mirror.

"It's not quite right," she admitted.

With that memory bright and clear in my mind, I decided that, yes, Phil *had* in fact worn the hated red dress to the charity auction. Moreover, she had, in fact, *always* worn it, and had never worn the delightful teal dress.

Across the ballroom, *he* guided Phil onto the dance floor as the DJ obligingly spun up a slow dance number, and Phil molded her body to *his*, molded her red-bedressed body to *his*, and swayed—the way she'd molded and swayed against me at our prom, only a year ago. My mouth turned Sahara; the tips of my fingers vibrated. The stench of chocolate syrup became overwhelming, strong and overly sweet.

"George." My voice sounded unlike my own, resonated throaty and vaporous. "George, look over at Phil."

"Dude. Please. Give it up. She's moved on. She's with *him* now, okay?" (He did not actually say *him*. He said instead *his* name—which I refuse to see or hear or record. My revenge, though small.)

Somehow he'd also managed to procure a half Diet Coke, half lemonade.

"Look at her dress, George."

"Dude, what about it?"

In the space of minutes, in the time from her entrance until now, Phil's dress had gone from relationship-souring red to fondly remembered and complementary teal and back again. And only I had noticed.

I could not speak. I stole George's half Diet Coke, half lemonade and drained the glass by half its remainder, thinking of Zeno and Achilles and a tortoise for a moment.[1]

"George." I gasped. "Do you remember when Phil came in? What I said?"

"Sure. You said, 'The red one is all wrong. She should have worn the teal.'"

I decided that Phil had worn the teal dress after all.

On the dance floor, she remained fused to *him* . . . in her teal dress. Less than a moment earlier, the dress had been red.

---

1. Zeno's paradox illustrates the essential impossibility of touching anything, using the image of Achilles chasing a tortoise. Of course, Achilles is much faster than a tortoise and should be able to catch it easily. But Zeno asks us to imagine that with each step he takes, Achilles halves the distance between himself and the tortoise. So, if the tortoise is ten feet away, the first step cuts the distance to five; the second step to two and a half; the third to one and a quarter; etc. But no matter how many steps Achilles takes, he will always be half of the previous distance away from the tortoise. Similarly, Mike will never finish the drink if he keeps halving the contents of the cup. (PROOFREADER'S NOTE: Zeno posed several paradoxes, but only three of them are really famous. The argument here is far closer to his Dichotomy paradox than to his Achilles and the Tortoise paradox. Though, in the end, they both get you to the same place—nowhere, at least relative to the target.)

George reached for his drink, but I ducked away and took another swig.

"Say it again," I commanded. "Tell me what I said when she came in."

He rolled his eyes. "Dude, the music isn't *that* loud. You said, 'I'm glad she wore the teal—that's the best one for her hair color.'"

Phil had worn the red, and had worn the teal—and not only that, she had always worn the red, and had always worn the teal. Only I noticed the difference in the *always*. So I thought about how it all started. I thought about the beginning.

I imagined it as the first chapter in my story, though of course it wasn't.

EMAIL EXCHANGE DOWNLOAD COMPLETE

FROM: THE AUTHOR
TO: THE EDITOR
SUBJECT: It's not working

OK, look, I know what you're trying to do here. I gave you an insanely huge book and you had the idea to whittle it down. And I appreciate your effort, but we're only one chapter in and look at what we've lost already!

FROM: THE EDITOR
TO: THE AUTHOR
SUBJECT: Re: It's not working

You are reading me wrong. I extracted the heart of the novel—Mike's relationship with Phil, and their relationship with *you*—from the morass you wrote, which is largely about yourself.

PART I

CHAPTER 1

"Do you want to hear something scary?" Phil asks.

We're entwined in her bed, one week before senior year begins.

"Tell me something scary."

"I think I'm falling in love with you," she says, shivering.

"I think I'm falling in love with you, too."

The truth is, I've been falling in love with Phil for weeks now.

Our relationship began with nothing dramatic: a party at George's house a month previous, a bored me in the garage–cum–game room as an equally bored Phil abandoned everyone else in the basement–cum–party room, on a quest for more wine coolers in the garage fridge. Meaningless small talk metamorphosed into a three-hour dialogue during which we—emotionally and physically—came closer and closer . . . until making out commenced on the rug, wine coolers long since consumed.

Phil had been a constant in my life, though a constant on the periphery.

The girl with the blue hair. It shimmered like sapphire when wet.

She'd transferred to our school in seventh grade, instantly captivating everyone with that air of insouciance, the mystique of that blue hair, the casual-yet-biting way she told teachers, "Phil," when they called out for "Philomel" during roll call. During that terrible middle school era, she'd also acquired the appearance of her namesake instrument: more angular than curvy (not in a bad way) slim waist, and a graceful neck. But all outward appearances, inexplicable or not, paled in comparison to her will. Almost single-handedly she willed into existence a pre-high-school-level drama club. She became a darling of parents and faculty by rallying the students to attend—*all* the students, including those who had expressed no interest at all in the dramatic arts. All were captivated by her insistent energy and unironic naiveté, which she rode into the lead role in nearly every high school play, as well as summer performances at the local college.

I'd never thought I had a chance with her. So I never even tried until the night of the wine coolers. Even then, she made the first move, sidling close enough that our thighs touched, hers under a denim skirt.

"You weren't supposed to say that," Phil says, annoyed. But she stays close. "You're not supposed to be falling in love with me."

"Why not?"

"Because we're almost seniors. Because you'll go away to college, and I'm going to stay here. Because."

"You don't know any of that," I say.

It's true: she doesn't know. She suspects I want to go to College Y[2] (also true), although I haven't decided, because I don't know if I'll get in.

The bigger truth is that we're in Phil's bed and I want to stop talking.

Phil's mom—perennially single, never married, Phil's dad long vanished—considers herself a "cool mom." She does not mind that her daughter and I have "safe sex" in her house, and on Phil's fifteenth birthday, stocked their shared bathroom with a variety pack of condoms. Still, Phil and I agree: "If your mom can hear your O noises, it's just way too creepy." (Phil's words.) Thus we abstain unless the house is empty. So when we hear Phil's mother's car in the driveway during the silence stretching between us, we pull apart.

2. No colleges are identified by name in this novel or in *Unedited*—for reasons the author never explained to his editor. Still, college anonymity was a conceit the editor found interesting, and therefore never questioned, as it makes a certain kind of sense in the broader context of both works. Readers, you are free to imagine colleges of your choice where identified by letter.

"Read to me," she says.

"What?"

"Read to me." Phil curls up and points to a wall-mounted shelf I have noticed several times, crammed with books: *The Wind in the Willows*, A. A. Milne, Beatrix Potter, and all the other venerable friends left behind in the old precincts of childhood when we packed our innocence onto a truck and moved to the new town of Growing Up. A sudden terror seizes me: Phil dated *him* almost from day one, holding hands with *him* from her second week in town until two days after the junior prom. The terror is such: Was this *his* ritual with her? Did *he* read to her from the volumes of her dad-present youth?

"I like the sound of your voice," she adds playfully. "I mean, I would love to hear about your underwater hotel[3] idea again, but I've heard it before. C'mon, Mike. I like being read to. Just pick one and read to me."

I imagine *him* in the same position, *him* next to her in bed, her curled toward *him* but not touching. (Did *he* have an ambitious project related to dreams of a future that *he* shared with her, denied so that *he* would read aloud?) *He* with legs outstretched, head propped up against the padded headboard, Milne open on *his* lap. *He* mimics a high falsetto for Pooh, a childish whisper for Roo, a downbeat-worded moan for Eeyore, et cetera. What are her expectations of me? Is it not enough that I am at her beck and call, that I attend to her every word, that I spend every moment not at work (delivering Indian food for a local restaurant or lifeguarding at the community pool) with her, that I have accompanied her on quotidian errands to the grocery store, the mall, the nail salon, the doctor's office, the dentist, all in the last two weeks alone? Now I am also her entertainment, her Man of a Thousand Voices?

"I'm not going to read to you," I say, demolishing with a single sentence any chance of comparison between *him* and me. "I'm not your parent."

She pouts. "Come on. Just one story. Not a whole book. A chapter."

---

3. Mike's idea for an underwater hotel was written before there were underwater homes in Dubai—mentioned only as evidence that reality often plays catch-up with fiction until the former (tragically or wonderfully) outpaces the latter.

"No. Stop it."

The possibility of *his* reading coils in a dark recess of my back brain, a quiescent snake of doubt. It is poisonous, ready to lunge and strike at the scantiest hint of comparison between me and *him*. For this reason, I cannot allow myself to read to her.

"You suck," she says lightly, flouncing on the bed, such that her dress flies up.

"Yeah, I suck. Why do you hate me so much?" I stretch out next to her and kiss her neck just below the ear, a spot I know makes her melt and shiver all at once.

"I don't hate you," she whispers, melting and shivering simultaneously. "I . . ."

There is nothing after "I . . ." except dead white space.

Well, that and her mother slamming the door and yelling, "I'm home!"

And then four months of Phil and me: a couple in the halls of high school senior year, oohed and aahed over by *her* friends, shoulder-punched by *my* friends, busted for PDAs between classes—and preparations for the senior play (Phil's swan song), together for long hours as I design the set—so that the end of each school day often finds the two of us collapsing against each other, snuggling momentarily in the wings before the custodians shut off the lights.

I am lucky. My parents have surrendered to the inevitability of my adulthood. As I close in on my eighteenth birthday, they no longer bother attempting to police my comings and goings with curfews and deadlines as long as my grades "stay up there, young man." They didn't gift me a bowlful of condoms, but I am free to do as I please.

"I should wash these sheets someday," Phil muses one late afternoon as we prepare to go downstairs.

"When was the last time you washed them?"

"Not since before we became a thing."

"Oh."

"The last time I washed them was right before the first time you came over," she said, unaware of both my panic and my instant relief.

"I wanted them nice and clean for you. I knew it was going to happen that night."

"You knew?" I had assumed nothing, grateful only that Phil, beautiful Phil, had seen fit to take me home.

"Duh. After the way we were all over each other in George's garage? Please. Did you really think I was going to deny myself after that?"

I want to ask: *Did you ever deny* him?

Instead, I think of the first time I saw her. Homeroom, seventh grade, first day of school. I was slumped and silent, a bony jumble of insecurity. She was upright and self-assured and utterly composed—at the head of the class, no less—ignoring the giggles and the undercurrent of chatter about her hair color.

Within a week, George reported spying her holding hands with *him* on the playground at recess.

CHAPTER 2

"Dude," George says.

We're on his rickety old deck. George is making his way through a six-pack of Stella Artois, "the only beer worth drinking," in his estimation. George's mother refuses to let him drink while underage and while living "under *my* roof!" so deck drinking is their uneasy compromise, placing George technically beyond the jurisdiction of "under *my* roof!" though not beyond the jurisdiction of law enforcement, whom his mother occasionally threatens to call.

"Dude, you're with her all the time," he goes on. "You in love or something? I figure you're gonna end up in the old-age home, chasing after her with your walker, you know what I mean?" He pauses, creasing his brow. "What will her hair look like when she gets old? You think it'll go gray or will it just get, like, lighter blue?"

"I don't know. I don't care."

"Cornflower? Periwinkle?"

"Seriously. Don't care."

"Powder blue? Robin's-egg blue? Ice blue?"

"George."

"Dude—" Here George belches with great intensity, as though determined to communicate some vital fact via carbon dioxide and methane. "You lack curiosity. That's your fatal flaw. Not hubris. Not cluelessness.

Curiosity, man. It killed the cat, but *lack* of it will kill *you*, you know what I mean? Trust me on this." He points the open mouth of his beer bottle at me.

To me, the mouth is like an eye: watching, staring, unblinking.

It makes me uncomfortable. I look away.

"I've always trusted you, George."

It's true. And he has always trusted me.

We bonded early, in grade school. George was the fatherless runt chosen last for games; I was the early-growth-spurted klutz and penulti-mate choice—my relative size compensating just barely for my complete lack of skill, poise, grace, and coordination.

"I will *never* be like the asshole," he says.

It's what he always says when I remind him that I trust him. And I appreciate it. Aside from me, he has said this only to his mother, school counselors, and a small army of therapists.

George refuses to speak his father's name. He refuses even to utter the words "my father" or "my dad" or any permutation of a first-person possessive pronoun and a paternal noun—referring to the asshole simply as "the asshole." Not even capitalized, for "the asshole doesn't deserve capital letters."

His first memory (and thus my most intense memory of George, though I was not there) is of the asshole knocking him down a flight of stairs with a kick to the shoulder. Years later, the police finally hauled the asshole away, but only after his mother tried to explain to an ER nurse why and how her young son had ended up with three broken fingers, a dislocated shoulder, and a suspiciously hand-shaped welt on his back . . . while at the same time *she* had suffered a black eye, a cracked molar, and significant bruising. What George suffered in those years (and, no doubt, in the years previous, prior to the advent of his memories) was sometimes even worse. Sometimes it was not as bad. But it was constant. Details and scenes have seeped out like tears on nights like these . . . George with a six-pack while I plead with him not to drink, having been secretly terrified of getting drunk for as long as I can remember.

For two years in my preadolescence, my parents' marriage teetered on the brink of divorce, threatening to topple me into that chasm on an almost daily basis. George, during this time, was my rock. To this day he insists that this relatively minor blip in my otherwise idyllic childhood somehow entitles me to equal standing with his father-beaten self, with no amount of cajoling, persuading, pleading, self-effacement, or outright insistence convincing him otherwise. All of this leads me to believe and to understand that a best friend is perhaps best defined as someone whose upbringing sucked vastly more than your own . . . and yet steadfastly contends that *your* upbringing was just as bad, if not worse.

By this particular logic George is my best friend, but I can never be his.[4]

"But I didn't mean to go off on the asshole again," he says. "Sorry, dude. How did I even start talking about him, anyway?" He smirks. "I've probably been reading too much Gayl Rybar."

He's giving me shit, so I raise a good-natured middle finger in return. Gayl Rybar is an author George loves—specifically of nonadult novels, about which I feel superior—and I have told him as much. As a future architect, I aim to be reading Ayn Rand and Don DeLillo.[5] Should I try to pretend like I care? Should I try to ask why Gayl Rybar is relevant to this conversation?[6] No, I shouldn't. George is baiting me, and it would be beneath both of us to take the bait.

"Anyway," he adds, "I figure you'll still be sticking it to the blue bombshell when you need the little blue pills, you know what I mean?"

One of George's more endearing traits is that he thinks he's more subtle than he actually is. Everyone *always* knows what he means.

"Yeah, I know what you mean, George."

My cell chirps its incoming text message alert.

---

4. For a deeper dive into George's miserable childhood, please refer to *Unedited*, chapter 2. Pages 26–27

5. I still haven't read either author, but I know (or have read) that architecture plays a vital role in Ayn Rand's *The Fountainhead* and Don DeLillo's *Zero*.

6. THE AUTHOR: Why *is* Gayl Rybar relevant to this conversation? What are you doing? Gayl isn't supposed to show up until much later! THE EDITOR: Just trust me. It'll all come together.

i wish i had gummi bears

"Dude, is the missus calling?" George leans back to get the last drops of beer, precariously close to toppling over the rail.

I resist the urge to shout for him to be careful. He hates being looked after, mothered, coddled. "Shut up," I tell him instead. "She's not the missus."

"Dude, you are *so* pussywhipped."

"So you keep telling me. It's the eighth time you've told me tonight."

He isn't listening. "I bet if I pulled down your pants right now, there wouldn't even be a dick there. You're smooth like Ken, you know what I mean? She has it all locked up in her hope chest, doesn't she?"

I slide my phone into my pocket.

"Dude, I don't get it," George continues. "I mean, yeah, she's hot. No question about it. And I guess the blue hair thing is kinda cool, but anyone can dye their hair. So what's so special about her? Why her?"

I set aside that Phil's hair is not dyed or otherwise artificially colored in any way. It is impossible for me to find the words that account for every level of Phil's distinction among girls—among human beings in general—as they have yet to be invented. Not that Phil herself is impossible to describe, but rather the intersection of the two of us . . . is indescribable: that coordinate point on the plane of space-time where the Platonic ideal of Phil-ness meets the Platonic ideal of Mike-ness. Explaining "Why Phil?" is like explaining "Why do babies love their mothers?" or "Why do dogs love their masters?" It simply *is*. There is no "because." But George will not—*cannot*—accept this.

And yet, when a best friend asks his friend, "Why her?" an answer must come forth, even if it is composed of bullshit. "Because she believes in me," I tell him. "She has always believed in me."

"Right, right." He grins. "This is all about your dreams of being a psychotic architect."[7]

---

7. Mike's architectural aspirations are relayed in great detail in *Unedited*, in various forms, especially on pages 104–115.

Of course it is decidedly *not* about that; it is about young Phil's defiant "Phil!" when called "Philomel." About self-assurance and self-confidence, projected.

"Shut up. No one else ever believed."

He slurps his beer. "I did. I *do*. You will open up entirely new frontiers in the field of psychotic architecture."

I open my mouth but hesitate. Yes, George does believe this. But while he believes *now*, in the here and now, the early days of our senior year of high school—and will continue to believe it a year from now, when we watch *him* dance with Phil—he never believed it *then* . . . before the beer, when we were kids and I first told him that I dreamed of designing a building that spun like a top and a housing development wherein each dwelling represented a sign of the Chinese Zodiac.

Phil believed in them all.

She believed in *me*, for reasons I have never understood nor sought to clarify. It never mattered why. Besides, right now, in the present tense, Phil is mine—and her belief about me is mine, too.

"Can I tell you something?" I tell George. (I tell, not ask, because despite the question mark, it isn't really a question; it's a prelude to a statement.) "I've been having . . . I've been having this weird sensation lately. Like remembering a dream, but I know I never dreamed it . . . I dreamed we were at a dance . . . Phil was with *him*."

"Dude, that's not a dream; that was junior prom. You know what I mean?"

And I do, and it was. But this dance is not junior prom; Phil is not sixteen-almost-seventeen. She is older. I am older. *He* is older.

"My thoughts have been weird lately. Like, I'm talking to you normally, but my thoughts are all complicated and wound up around themselves."

"That's because you're a complicated, wound-up-around-yourself kinda guy, Mikey."

I laugh.

"You let yourself get complicated," he tells me. "It's like with Phil:

You can't just be in a relationship. You have to obsess over it. You have to wallow in it."

"Are you saying I shouldn't be with her?"

"I'm not saying anything. I'm just saying . . . Dude, you're complicated because you made the decision to be complicated."

"I don't know if that's true."

"Can I tell *you* something?" he asks.

I look at him. This is different; he wants my permission. "Go ahead."

George gathers his thoughts, conflicted. "I've never told you this before," he says. "I've never told anyone. I don't know why I'm telling you now. I have three secrets. I'll tell you the first two, but I'll never tell you the third."

I'm uncertain how to react. It all sounds vaguely familiar to me.

"Just one of the two for now," he says. He upends the bottle for a protracted moment, longer than it takes to drain the last of the beer within . . . stalling. Then he sets the bottle down. Without meeting my eyes, he continues: "When I was six, I woke up one night. Late in the night. Early in the morning. Same thing, you know what I mean? I woke up because I'd heard a noise. Or maybe I dreamed that I'd heard a noise. I don't know."

"You were afraid someone was breaking into the house."

He laughs. "No. I was never afraid of that. The asshole was already in the house. Why would I be afraid of someone breaking in?"

Right. I should have known and understood that; I should have intuited that.

"But I heard something. Or I thought I heard something, or dreamed I heard something. I woke up, thinking that the asshole was hurting Mom again—because he was *always* hurting Mom, always hurting me, and, like, I never did anything about it. Never even *thought* of doing anything about it. But that night I just got up out of bed and went into the kitchen, and the next thing I knew, I was standing outside my parents' bedroom, holding the big knife we use to carve Thanksgiving turkey. And it was dead quiet there. The knife in my hands—I was six, dude, you know what I mean?—the knife looked like a fucking machete. I couldn't hear anything at all. He wasn't hitting her. She didn't need me to protect her. But I opened the door anyway. I held my breath. I was quiet. I think it took five minutes to open that door, turning the knob slowly so it wouldn't make any noise, easing the door open . . . you know what I mean? It was dark. I went to the asshole's side of the bed. He was snoring, lying on his back, and Mom was curled up next to him, and if you looked at them . . . Dude, you'd think they were normal and regular and happy, you know what I mean? And I think maybe they were like that. Happy, I mean. *Then*. I mean, when they were asleep, they were like everyone else in the world. Does that make any sense?"

I nod, even though he isn't looking at me.

"And I stood there, and I held the knife about an inch away from his neck. The artery, right here, what's it called?[8] Just about an inch. I could have sliced right through him, right into him, and he would have bled out pretty fast. I knew that. Even then. All those movies he used to let me watch . . . I knew." He shakes his head, still not looking at me. "And then I went and I snuck out and I closed the door and I put the knife back and I went to bed like nothing had happened. Fell right asleep."

"You were scared to act," I say.

In the pause that follows, I realize that perhaps I do not know George as well as I'd thought. He shakes his head again and looks at me—his eyes troubled, his face tight with shame and guilt and pain. "I wasn't afraid. Not of him, not of anything. Still not, you know what I mean? It's just that . . . It's just that I realized, standing there, I realized that I loved him. After all that shit and all the shit I knew would come, I still loved him. You know what I mean?"

For the first time in our friendship, I do not know what he means. All I know is that he survives, as he always has. And I know that a year from now George—no worse for wear—will attend the Wallace-Barth School charity ball with me and drink a glass of half lemonade, half Diet

---

8. He means the carotid, but I say nothing.

Coke. But whether I answer, or whether he's lying about his fear, I do not know. In a way I don't care, either. This part is over.

At home, my parents watch TV while my younger brother practices his harmonica/flute/trombone/piano.

He badgers me to listen as he plays Dylan/Beethoven/Sousa/Brahms.

I listen for longer than it takes to produce a sentence saying so. The experience is unmemorable, leaving no sensory impressions to speak of. Nothing to report.

He finishes with a flourish, and I applaud, and he says something endearingly funny, but in no way reminiscent of a younger sibling on a sitcom.

I go to my room.

Inside are my things. My belongings. Things that belong to me.

A bed—where I sleep. A dresser—where I store my clothes. A desk—where I do my homework. A bookshelf—where there sits a framed picture of Phil . . . yet for some reason whose contents, book-wise, I cannot describe.

I lie on my bed, and I wonder what is happening to me.

And then the page turns.

CHAPTER 3

When I was younger, I had an affliction that caused me to narrate my own life story. Not out loud, but internally. Always in the third person, as though some secondary editorial personality had taken up residence inside my head.

He walked down the school corridor, I would think while walking down the school corridor, *dodging his fellow students while on his way to science class*, while dodging my fellow students on my way to science class. When I said, "Good morning," to my mother, I would add a silent *he said* afterward. The self-narration blossomed like a genetically mutated flower that doesn't open its petals over time, but instead bursts instantaneously into full bloom. So maybe more like an explosion. No, the flower of madness was alive inside me; an explosion is a temporal event, not a living thing. Maybe it was less like a flower and more like a hermit crab that seeks shelter in a new shell, without realizing that another hermit crab already calls this particular shell home . . . of course, the correct organism analogy doesn't really matter. Only the madness does.

I did not *want* to narrate my life. I did not *want* to imagine quotation marks during conversation with friends, enemies, parents, or teachers (judiciously adding dialogue tags when required); above all, I did not want to describe every moment of my day in a way that I—Mike, me, MYSELF—wouldn't. *He brushed his teeth, white foam spilling from between his lips as though he'd bitten into a soapy sponge.* Or: *He lay in bed, tossing and turning, as unable to sleep as a man who expects surgery in the morning.* (Bad enough I had a writer living in my skull; he/she/it was a bad enough writer, too!) I had no choice, though. I could find no way to prevent this narration. My consciousness had been hijacked.

After a few months, I considered telling my parents. But I found that avenue blocked by a series of walls, each higher than the previous.

First Wall: How do I describe this affliction? I imagined beginning with *There's a narrator in my head*, triggering gasps of shock, looks of alarm, and cries of *You hear voices in your head?* followed, no doubt, by a visit to a psychiatrist . . . and then what? Even at that young age, I was pretty certain that the voice in my head was merely annoying, not dangerous; I also knew that I wouldn't be able to convince a doctor of this certainty.

Second Wall: But what if it *was* dangerous? Perhaps this was how schizophrenia started, with harmless babble that later evolved into full-blown lunacy. I'd believed it to be a flower in full bloom; in truth, it was a bud that had yet to open. Or a hermit crab with superpowers. If I was losing my mind, I wasn't sure I wanted to know.

Third Wall: Conversely, what if I wasn't alone? What if this just happened? Maybe this state was entirely, boringly normal and mundane. Maybe *everyone* had a narrator's voice nestled deep within the gray matter—a calm and reasoned influence (for my voice was both, never excitable or agitated or even mildly aroused) on the day in and day out. What if, in fact, my internal voice indicated a personal flaw not by dint of its mere existence, but rather by dint of its late arrival? What if I sat down with my parents to tell them about this new presence in my brain and they responded, in hushed tones of panic, *"You mean . . . you've been going along all these years* without *your internal narrator?"*

There was no Fourth Wall, but none was needed.

The Third Wall frightened me and intrigued me more than the others; it was the most difficult to climb. I was always something of a daydreamer, given to disappearing into my own thoughts for extended periods, usually about a place. Both George and Phil were aware of this, my architectural wormhole, my fantasizing rigid Doric columns and enormous vaults and innovative uses for geodesic domes and the artistry of the fine crenellations at the tops of towers and keeps . . . only to realize later that time had passed, the world had moved on, things had *happened*—all of which I'd been completely unaware of. Was it possible that, somehow, I had tuned out on one crucial day: the Day the Narrative Voice Is Explained? Or what if it required no explanation at all? Maybe I was defective because I felt the voice as alien presence (a flower, a squatting hermit crab), while the rest of humanity coexisted peacefully with their internal narrators—without stress, strain, or disturbance?

Ultimately, after many thousands of unwritten words of narration, the cure came (as is the case with so many childhood maladies) with a dose of mortal embarrassment.

School had ended. The community pool—chaos incarnate, the only relief from the heat other than air-conditioning, a refuge for stir-crazy families who could not abide the idea of being cooped up—had opened for the summer. I went with George, who dove in immediately. I shucked off my flip-flops (*He shucked off his flip-flops*) and ran to the pool (*and ran to the pool*) as George shouted, "What are you waiting for?" already splashing and relieved.

"'Here I come!' he yelled," I yelled.

Out loud.

My internal narrator, my private verbal shadow, had just spoken *out loud*. Attributing my own dialogue to me. In the air. To the world.

I was midleap, poised to plunge into the deep end. I had just enough time to contemplate this breach of etiquette, propriety, and possibly sanity before I hit the water. I assumed I would dissolve. But I didn't. The cool water enveloped me, and I rose with the fizz of my plunge, broke the surface for breath, rising into the cacophony and mayhem.

George paddled over. "Dude!" he gasped. "You totally nailed that bald guy with your splash! It was awesome."

I looked around. No one had noticed. No one had heard me over the raucous sounds of a community at play. But that moment of shame still stuck in me like a dart. Apparently, the shock of it had killed the narrator's voice, for I never heard it again. So while my current predicament is not the same, I am still certain:

Something is happening.

Something is coming.

I feel it.

But this part of the story is over.

It's a weekend. It would have to be; hence George's drinking last night. I wouldn't stay up and he wouldn't drink if it were a school night, would I/he? And it's afternoon, hot outside. I need to talk to my brother. That way I can determine if my "complicated" thoughts have made their way back into my speech. My conversation with George last night wasn't a true conversation; it was an exchange between friends in a private vernacular. It's not an adequate test to determine if this long-dormant flower / hermit crab has reappeared.

When I find my brother at his computer, I am relieved to hear myself say, "Hey, bro, what's up?" in the usual casual, affectedly unaffected tones of late teenage-dom. It is the proof I sought: my external dialogue is normal and natural; only my internal monologue suffers from a peculiar variation of stiltedness, formality, periphrasis. I feel a wave of relief.

Plus, it's good to reconnect with my younger brother.

As it turns out, he has a crush. And since I once had a crush on Phil—a crush that morphed into romance, then into love—I am able to offer him advice, both brotherly and manly, thereby showing that I am a sympathetic, good-hearted person. In a word, likable. Likability being of prime importance, of course, mattering more than curiosity or interest or surprise or passion. But let us not forget: this is a story about Phil and a story about me and, occasionally, a story about Phil and me and all the world, as well.

My brother thanks me by saying something ironic and insightful that bears on both my current relationship with Phil and my future with her.

I thank him in return.

Phil texts:

I'm walking up your driveway.

We have a date tonight. *Date* feels like an outmoded word and concept, yet we plan to have dinner and see a movie, which qualifies as a *date* no matter the time period.

When the doorbell rings, I race downstairs.

Phil is wearing a dress I love. It is teal. (Her word.) Teal is . . . what, exactly? Blue, but with a hint of green. The color of the ocean where I imagine my underwater hotel. It's also oddly formal. Why is she wearing it? Not that I mind; she looks good in it. But before I can ask, I realize—*Shit*—I left my cell phone in my room by accident. Yes, I am phone-obsessed—it is the albatross around my neck—but I also respect my parents' authority. Even though I am seventeen-soon-eighteen, my parents have a rule: when out of the house for any purpose other than school, I am to have my cell phone with me and on at all times. So I kiss her lightly and go to my room. Phil lounges in the kitchen while waiting for me. My brother says hello from the top of the stairs. Phil says hello back. My cell sits atop a pile of sketchbooks and drawings on my desk. I retrieve it and run back down to the front door, calling out to Phil that I am ready.

When she does not come to the door, I call out again. And then a third time. Nothing.

I go to the kitchen.

She sits at the table, an envelope in her hands.

"Phil. Come on. Let's go."

No response.

"Phil."

Wordlessly, she turns the envelope to me. I recognize the crest of College Y. "Oh. Oh." Guilt falls over me like a shadow. For not only have I requested admissions materials from College Y, but I also did so surreptitiously, keeping it a secret from Phil.

"It's admissions information," she says in a flat voice, as though she needs to explain this fact to me. She does not.

"I didn't ask for that," I tell her. "My parents sent away for that. I told them I wasn't interested in going to Y anymore, but they didn't listen."

"They didn't listen."

"Right. I'm totally not even applying there. Don't worry about it."

"They sent away for it."

"Right." Why does she keep stating the obvious?

Her face is inscrutable, framed by her blue hair. Slowly—far more slowly than I would have even thought possible—she returns the envelope to the pile of mail on the kitchen table. Together we go to the subway, the issue done and over with.

Or so I believe, until later, tangled in the unlaundered sheets that preserve a record of our history (though still history in the making at this point), when she says to me, "Why would your parents send away for the stuff from College Y if you told them you didn't want to go?"

"Phil, I'm not lying. I seriously told them that. And I'm not going there. I told you: I'm not even going to apply."

"I believe you, but why would they do it?"

I have no answer. I must have misread the situation entirely.

Eyes dull with regret, she says, "They did it because they know how badly you want to go there."

"Phil—"

"Stop. Let me finish. They know how badly you want to go. They know because it's all you've ever talked about. Ever since you were a kid. Ever since you wanted to be an architect. You knew. You've always known that's what you wanted. And they've always known that that's what you've known because you told them. Again and again. At first—"

"Phil, come on," I interrupt. "I don't . . ." My voice peters out with her glare.

She continues: "At first, they probably didn't take you seriously because no one ever takes kids seriously. But the years went by and you never wavered. You never changed your mind. You kept telling them, 'I want to be an architect, and College Y has the best program for architecture, so I want to go there.' You said it over and over. And they believed you."

I throw my hands up. "So what? They can't admit I changed my mind. They're parents! My dad still thinks I love pudding pops because I used to eat a box of them every week."

"Mike. This isn't fucking pudding pops, okay? This is about your dreams and your future. *You* can't admit it. It's ingrained in you. You've held on to this dream since you were a little kid. For *years*. That doesn't just go away. That doesn't just stop."

I'm silent. I want to tell her: Y isn't the only school for architecture. There are plenty of programs around here. Even at State. My dream is to be an architect, not specifically an architecture student at College Y.

We are silent for eternities.

Those silent eternities are still in the future, though.

I live only four subway stops from Phil's house. On our way back to her house, I spend the time on the train thinking about the future. In my dream/vision/hallucination of the future, I see Phil reunited with *him*, molded to *him* on the dance floor at a charity function of some sort, but in a dress that is not teal. A dress that is red: the one she tried on for the prom. As mentioned, I hate that dress.

I cannot shake this image, cannot write it off as the useless psychic flotsam and jetsam of a night's sleep.

George thinks it is simply a sub/unconscious (he is unsure of the correct term, psychoanalytically speaking) fear of losing Phil. I know this because I remember something. I am only remembering it now. Last night, in that blank space, George said something to me:

"I learned in psych last year that in a dream, *every character is you*. So you weren't really dreaming about *him* taking Phil away from you. You were dreaming about losing *yourself* to some *other* aspect of yourself . . . you know what I mean?"

To which I replied, "George, that's crap." I left it that because, at the time, I was convinced that I'd seen a true vision of the future.

"The future is crap," George told me in return. "And that means the future is easy."

CHAPTER 4

When we arrive at Phil's house, the first thing I notice is that her mother's car is not in the driveway.

Our date was strained and restrained. Dinner—Belgian food, of course—was subpar. Yet neither of us felt like complaining, so maybe that's why the issue of College Y dissipated.

But here we are at her house, her motherless house. Which usually means one thing.

And still does.

As, I race upstairs, chasing Phil, I hear her laugh. I laugh, too.

So maybe George is at least half right. The future, at least as far as right now is concerned, is easy.

Afterward—wrapped in the history-made sheets, her teal dress lying in a heap on the floor, staring at the ceiling fan buzzing above—I cannot imagine that Phil will ever *not* be with me. I summon gooseflesh on her exposed shoulder. My touch is irrefutable proof. She will never be with *him* again, molded to *him*, red dress or teal dress. Whichever dress . . .

Still, I wonder.

Did that happen? Did I imagine it? Is it yet to come?

We've never spoken of *him*, not once, and so I want to ask her if she would ever want to go back—

"That was art," she murmurs.

"I'm an artsy guy," I say drolly. "I create things."

She laughs. "In a scientific way. You design. You're not artsy like drama-artsy or writer-artsy. Have you ever read *The Faerie Queene*? By Spenser?"

"Mmm . . ." I have a vague memory of these words being mentioned in a similar order in an English class of some sort.

"It starts, 'A Gentle Knight was pricking on the plaine,'" she says triumphantly.

I wait for her to go on. But that's it. Maybe the conversation is over.

"So? What about it?"

"Don't you understand? Pricking. It's archaic. Means 'riding' or something like that."

I am halfway toward a dirty pun involving the word "prick" and the notions of mounting and riding, but she interrupts with a fierce shake of her head.

"No, it means more than that. Don't you get it?"

"No. Not really."

"A prick can be, okay, a colloquialism for . . . whatever. But it's a verb, too, right? 'Urging on.' It's utterly omnisexual, this word. It's about the sexes and about the act of sex, okay? And then . . . and then, if you just sort of . . . allegorize it . . . or analogize it . . . I'm not sure. But if you take the sexual connotation out of it? Then it means *any* action. *And* the actor. *And* the acted upon. So you end up with a knight who's pricked into pricking by a prick, thus turning him into a prick."

I turn to her. I have no idea what she's talking about. "What?"

Phil is staring at the ceiling, speaking as if a prerecorded explanation has been implanted inside her larynx: "Words can't be defined. They're a result of coincidence, not design. So the sequence of words is inconsequential because any word can mean any other word."

I frown. "Angia, what in the world—"

Angia?

Phil is not Angia; she's Phil.

Angia is someone else, someone who only (might have) existed in a dream—or, to use Phil's logic, *someone who cannot be defined*—because in reality, Angia is only a word that seems to have come from nowhere.

Phil is flesh. She is real. But for a moment she was as unreal as Angia is or was, and before I can apologize for using the wrong name, she shakes me off.

"Wait—wait," I stammer. "What just happened here?"

"Nothing. We're just talking." Her tone is light.

"About what?"

She giggles. "Man, architects are too damn serious. Probably because they know they could kill a thousand people if they put the floor in the wrong place."

"Why do you hate me?" I joke, as if by reflex.

"I don't hate you," she says. "It's just . . . I—I—"

I take the liminal moment between this word and the next.

Phil has said this to me many times. It was the banter equivalent of the soundtrack to our relationship. We joked about it. Or, rather, *I* joked about it. I felt, each time, that she had something more to say beyond *I don't hate you*, but each time I was more concerned with my need to make certain she understood I was joking. Was that because I knew what she meant to say? Or what she wanted to say? Did I somehow fear knowing the truth? Did I fear the complexity of it?

All of these things are true or may be true or probably/possibly are true.

I wait, and this time I don't interrupt. She stops anyway.

"No," I tell her. "Say what you were going to say."

She has something more to say—the words swim in her gaze—but she flops back on her pillow, a lighter blue than her own hair. "You didn't bring me gummi bears last night."

Caught off guard, my gears grinding at the change of topic and the downshifting of emotion, I blurt out, "You didn't ask for them."

"You dummy. I texted you."

"You just said you wanted them. You didn't say you wanted *me* to *bring* them to you."

"Oh, I see. So when you say, 'I'm horny,' you're just imparting information. I'm not supposed to act on it or anything." This is accompanied by a peck on the cheek to mitigate the sting. "Make it up to me; read to me." She points to the shelf.

"Come on, Phil. You know how to read."

"But I like it. And I like your voice."

"I'll feel like an idiot. They're little kid books."

"They're classics."

"Please. Even my little brother is too old for these. They're only classics because they don't *totally* suck and aren't *completely* boring, just *mostly* boring."

She pouts.

"Don't do that. I can't resist when you pout, and I really don't want to read to you."

"Why? You got something better to do today?"

At times—again, like this one—I can't help but to think back to our first time in bed, where my inability to read to her first exposed itself, even as we exposed ourselves to each other.

"We need to get up," she says abruptly.

"Why?"

She extricates herself from me with depressing ease, rolling off the mattress, her form sleek and agile and silent. "Help me strip the bed."

It's late afternoon. On a weekend. Her mom isn't home. The request makes no sense.

"What?"

"I said, 'Help me strip the bed,'" she repeats. Her voice is casual, as though she has not just made a decision that ends history.

I stare at the history-made sheets, twisted and wrapped around themselves, and I imagine that I can see each smudge, smear, blotch, and stain not as mere remnants of our romance—but rather as points on a timeline, an unspooled thread stretching back months and ending at this exact moment.

"Are you . . . are you going to wash them?" The question stumbles from my mouth.

She fixes her gaze on me. "Did you think I was going to put them under glass in a museum somewhere?"

"Well . . . no. But—"

"Then c'mon. Help me."

She tugs at the top sheet, popping it loose from the corner nearest her. After a moment, I follow suit, and together we peel back the record of our relationship until the bedclothes lie in a haphazard pile at our feet. I am quiet. I don't want to be quiet, but I am unable to articulate my exact concern. While I have always thought of the history-made sheets as a metaphor for our relationship and its longevity, I have never directly spoken to Phil about this, and so I do not know how now to ask her if there is any significance to stripping the bed. I feel as though merely asking her will break whatever spell the history-made sheets have spun, but then realize in the same instant that if there has been a spell woven by the sheets, then surely it is broken now anyway.

"Why are we doing this? I thought you would leave them on the bed as . . ." *As long as we were together. Because that's what you did with . . .*

I don't say the words, but Phil looks at me as though I have completed the thought, as though I haven't left the sentence dangling.

She pulls on a sweatshirt she never wears outside, emblazoned with the WB logo—i.e., our school's logo. (Phil and I, and George, of course—and *he*, of course—attend the Wallace-Barth School, the WB.) She slips into a wispy pair of panties that may as well not even exist. She brushes a strand of blue hair out of her eyes.

Her expression tells me nothing.

I stare down at the rumpled mass on the floor.

"Are you breaking up with me?" I ask dumbly, unable to look up.

In the silence I begin to wonder if she has somehow managed to leave the room. I think of Schrödinger's cat. As long as I don't look up, there is a chance that Phil is no longer present, a chance equal to the likelihood that she is still *in* the room. If she is not in the room, then she cannot say that she is breaking up with me.

I look up; the cat dies.

Phil is staring at me.

"Staying for dinner?" she asks, her tone dark and fathomless.

I can't answer. I don't know how.

"I know you have to work on your college apps," she answers for me. Then she pecks me on the lips, chastely, like a sister. "Have fun."

CHAPTER 5

My parents aren't quirky or dramatic. They aren't ex-hippies or ex-felons. They aren't ex-anything, really, except for ex–young people. Dad turned forty six weeks ago. He did not celebrate with a new Maserati, fake hair, or a Vegas "mancation." At thirty-nine, Mom is naturally gray and uninterested in dyeing; she is mostly interested in keeping busy. They have no bizarre or all-consuming hobbies; there is no room in our house set aside for a massive model-train garden. My mother does not experiment with arcane quinoa recipes. She does not host an erotic book club night, nor does she sign me up for leftist youth groups in a vicarious fight for social justice. My father does not call me "sport," does not regale me with endless stories in an embarrassing/amusing attempt at father-son bonding, does not keep his college uniform/glove out back in a toolshed-turned-shrine-to-lost-youth. Neither drinks to excess; still, they are not teetotalers. Neither has ever been cruel or abusive, has ever come close to lashing out with words or fists; that said, they are not afraid of discipline. They enforce no curfew, though they expect to know where I am.

In short, there is nothing to say about my parents other than that they are pleased to see me home so early on a Saturday night.

I typically spend this time at Phil's house. In her bed. Et cetera.

When I remind them about the applications, they are even happier.

I work at the computer, shuffling the papers and applications that have sat on my desk in a stack for weeks now, semiorganized by the school's desirability and ease of application. For a moment, I consider the state university, but I discard the notion with a swiftness I hope Phil will never be able to sense. She is convinced that the state university is in *her* future. So I must, perforce, at least consider it, but my consideration is so fleeting that it makes me wonder if Phil would deem that fleetness in direct proportion to my caring for her, which it most definitely is not . . .

I just can't see myself going to State.

I find my letters of recommendation, sealed in envelopes and stamped with the familiar WB logo by teachers who gave me good grades. I reflect that it's a convenient time to leave this school behind. For the past few years a rumor has hung in our halls like a fetid odor—that the WB is on the decline and fated to merge soon with another local private school, one that is smaller and less prestigious but renowned for its cutting-edge educational philosophy and award-winning staff. The goal is to boost enrollment by appealing to a new demographic of younger parents; the result will be a stronger, hipper school—a combined juggernaut to be dubbed Consolidated Wallace, or the CW.

This rumor bothers me only slightly, in that if it comes to pass, my alma mater will, in effect, vanish, leaving me with a diploma from a school that no longer exists save for the actual physical buildings . . . which are attractive and functional, but in no sense exceptional or memorable—at least, not in any historical or architectural context, which are the only contexts that matter to me.

I work on the apps and essays until dinner, which I consume with my family at the kitchen table. I listen to my brother's humorous anecdotes about his best friend / female crush / pet turtle. I return to my room and the applications—only to be interrupted the chirp of a text.

its raining out - come snuggle w/me & listen
2 the rain

Phil, of course. She loves listening to the rain on the rooftop. With rain so rare in the desert, fleeting when it comes at all, she loves to lie in the dark, lullabied by a liquid timpani—the harder the rain, the cozier the shelter—especially, "best of all" (her words), if there's a warm, strong body to curl up next to.

I have been so preoccupied with the applications that I haven't noticed the rain. I turn to the window, and I see that it is coming down in torrents. I would get soaked if I left the house. So I ignore the text, as I ignored the implicit request for gummies last night, and plunge back into my paperwork. For a moment I wonder why I even want to attend college, why *anyone* wants to attend college—thinking that, perhaps, it would be best if the world just didn't need it, if we could somehow survive without it . . . that if college didn't exist, life would maybe, possibly, somehow be perfect.

When I am too tired to concentrate anymore, I go to bed.

The hallway outside my bedroom is made of ice. All of it: floor, ceiling, walls. Strangely, I'm not cold, though I'm wearing only shorts and a T-shirt. But my breath produces the usual white puffs, a detail I always notice in the cold.

In the background, someone plays what sounds like an electric cello. A woman is accompanying *a contralto*, her voice warbly: *Hey, can you peel shrimp? Oh yeah, baby, gotta peel the shrimp.*[9] At the end of the hallway, where there should be an archway leading to the kitchen, I find only a wooden door set flawlessly into the surrounding ice.

When I grasp the doorknob, the woman's voice warns, *Not on the first date!*

Oh, I say. I reach for the doorknob again.

9. There are no quotation marks in dreams . . . Which you would know if you were reading *Unedited* instead of this bowdlerized version of the story. (EDITOR: Barry, I know you're upset about some of the editing, but please don't take it out on this book. Copy editor, please delete this footnote.)

NO! the voice shouts.

Why not? I whine, quite against my will.

The door vanishes, revealing not the kitchen but an extended corridor beyond; ice gives way to rough-hewn wood, askew and atilt, such that I'm forced to walk at an angle. I wonder at the mad architect who built this place. From nowhere, a man's voice sounds out: *But we weren't characters. And none of it made any sense. And, truthfully, that drove me a little bit crazy . . .*

The corridor opens into a large parlor room—lushly carpeted, paneled in oak, thankfully square and true. A fire roars in the fireplace. The mantelpiece seems conspicuously barren, as if waiting for framed pictures or knickknacks or family souvenirs, but unable to understand that they will never come, unable to learn to live with that sadness.

A man lies supine on the rug beside the fire. He's about my dad's age, if I had to guess. He wears jeans, battered black leather dress shoes, a shirt the color of old red wine in a dusty bottle, and a black jacket. Around his neck, a lanyard dangles, a plastic name badge winking in the firelight at its terminus.[10] I approach him quietly, on tiptoe, but as I near him, I see my caution is unnecessary. His eyes are closed. He's not breathing. He's *dead*, a certainty that fills me with a blend of horror and despair, even though I am equally certain I have never seen him before. My eyes rove over his slack face, his pale skin obscured by bland brown stubble that thickens to a beard at the chin. I have no idea who this man is. And yet as I drop to my knees next to his body, I fight back tears. I fumble for the name badge, convinced it can reveal all—but the letters are scrambled, the way letters can be in dreams, wherein no matter how strenuous the effort the underlying words remain indecipherable.

I was too late, I tell him. *I was too late. I couldn't save you.*

He opens his eyes and sits up. *Hey, Mike,* he says. *How are you?*

I'm . . . This isn't right. You're dead.

---

10. Here "terminus" is used to mean "an endpoint," though expecting its architectural denotation—that of a figure of a human bust or an animal springing forth from a square pillar, used to delineate a boundary in ancient Rome—would be understandable, given Mike's professed desire to someday be an architect.

Not always. Remember the tale of Angia Eiphon. The tale. The meta-phor. The allegory. The cautionary tale. She may be all of them.

Who's Angia Eiphon?

You'll need to go to sleep. You'll need to have a dream-within-a-dream.

I shake my head at his gibberish. What sort of name is Angia Eiphon, anyway? He's got a point. It does sound like something someone would dream . . . in the sort of dream where the dreamer walks down a street not far from his house, a street that he sees every day in his travels (to work? school? prison? who knows?) but is somehow foreign. On this familiar road made unfamiliar, the dreamer happens upon a house that in the waking world does not exist. But there is nothing sinister about this house.

Understand this. Know it like you know your name. There is noth-ing whatsoever sinister about this house. It is not a subconscious replay of a haunted house story, nor is it a Jungian projection of an archetypal fear of the unknown, nor is it a metaphor for the dual nature of homes: places that we feel compelled to flee and yet seek out in all our walks of life.

Understood. It's just a house.

The dreamer enters, moving through the rooms like a ghost, seeing but not touching. The memorabilia of its inhabitants might as well be a collection of alien artifacts. He cannot decipher the elaborately random codes, the way the items are arranged, the way one picture stands in the center of others, the way the couch tilts this way rather than that, one cushion in particular flattened and pushed out of shape by repeated use. Here, in these and a thousand other details, lies everything: entire histo-ries, personalities, losses, desires, tragedies, inside jokes—the gestalt—of the family. All of it at his fingertips. All of it inaccessible.

Out on the back porch, sunlight washes down on him down like rain.

The dreamer is no longer alone. The girl is here, too . . . in a pretty sundress, smile radiant, hair golden, eyes sparkling—her entire existence a cliché, which is fine because she is, after all, only a dream.

What's your name? the dreamer asks.

Angia Eiphon, she replies.

He loves her. Even though he has never loved before—even though he cannot recognize the sensation of this emotion—he knows this. He loves her. He will grow up to destroy her, to turn his own dream into a nightmare. He will do this because he has given himself no choice.

Angia Eiphon, he whispers, and vanishes.

Here I wake from the dream-within-a-dream, coming alive again only to watch the stubbly man's eyes close. He falls back, dead. Again. And I still understand nothing. I stand just as a child steps into the room, wearing shorts and a T-shirt, his body a strange, vibrating disruption of the air, as though he cannot be totally present. He holds a wireless microphone in one hand. A spotlight pins him.

Look, Mike! He gestures with his right hand, holding the microphone aloft. *Look, mic! I'm going to give you a glimpse, okay? Pay attention! There are no quotation marks in dreams, remember? You gotta remember something else for me, too, Mike. He's just a figment of his own imagination. Can you remember that?*

I think so, I say, looking down at the dead-again man.

I turn to the child and suddenly recognize him: I have seen him on the subway with a vanilla ice cream cone. But where, when? His microphone turns into that same ice cream cone, only not vanilla anymore. Now it's dripping with chocolate syrup. I double over, retching at the smell. It fills the room as the child smiles with chocolate-slick teeth. I need to get out of here.

Rooms don't always have one exit, Mike. And houses have many rooms. This is very architectural of me, wouldn't you say? Wouldn't you agree that this contributes to the architecture theme?

I can't reply. I can't even breathe.

I'm supposed to warn you about Inframan. But I'll tell you a secret, Mike: I am Inframan. So why would I warn you about myself?

Chocolate syrup has somehow become lodged in my gullet. I'm sure of it. I can taste it in the back of my throat and smell it from somewhere behind my nose.

Never . . . heard . . . of . . . him . . . I manage to choke out.

Of course not! But you know about Gayl Rybar. Am I right? You think I'm here to tell you things you know?

With that, the boy vanishes, and with him the stench of chocolate and the viscous mass inside my throat. I suck in air like a vacuum.

The dead man sits up again. *I'm going to tell you the future. I'm going to tell you what's on pages yet to be written. You will walk through the wreckage of a broken heart.*[11] *You will need to find me, all of me. Can you remember that?*

I've been asked to remember a lot. *Maybe.*

Well, make sure you do. It's important.

Is it?

You think I'm making this stuff up? I'm not making this stuff up. I'm making up other stuff. I've made up other stuff. Similar stuff, but not the same. Mike, you need to understand that you're not the first Mike. You're not the first one to go through this. This has been attempted before, but unsuccessfully. He . . . he loves that.

Who's he?

Der Untermensch. The Underone. The God of Failure. Inframan.

Why do I keep smelling chocolate syrup? Where is that coming from?

The man looks down, fingering his name badge. *My name is scrambled,* he says. Under the plastic, I see not a name, but a phrase: CLEAN IS MY ANAGRAM.

Look, Mike, the future is decided, but not written, he adds. *The future is going to happen. And you aren't ready, because you haven't finished your college apps, which you aren't capable of finishing, because there's something important you don't know. Isn't this all so very ~~Twin Peaks Lost Westworld~~ Twin Peaks?*

I DON'T UNDERSTAND!

Of course you don't. How can you? It's your own life—

The ringing of my phone wakes me up.

"Goddamnit!" I roll over, stretching out for the phone on the nightstand, all inchoate rage—at being close to understanding something in the dream, and instead blearily spotting Phil on my caller ID.

---

11. I hate to be a downer, but . . . this doesn't even happen in this book! It happens in *Unedited*, though, and it is weird and creepy and awesome!

"What?" I growl.

She hesitates just long enough to make me wonder if she's hung up on me before she says, "I . . ." and stops, then catches her breath. Without heat, without anger, without passion, she wearily adds, "Fuck you. I was calling to apologize."

"I'm sorry," I tell her reflexively. "I was asleep. I had a weird dream—"

"I don't . . . Look, I don't want to fight, okay? I'm sorry I woke you up."

"Accepted. There, apology accepted." I swallow.

"That's not what I'm calling to apologize about."

Right. I must admit, the idea of waking me up to apologize for waking me up seems enormously sensible in the wake of my dream. I am too confused to do anything but fall back on an old standby in order to salvage this conversation: "Why do you hate me?"

"I don't hate you," she automatically assures me. "I—I just . . ." Her voice trembles. "I just wanted . . . I've been thinking. Ever since you left. I've been thinking and thinking, and I keep thinking about that time we were in my bed—that early time, back right before school started, and I told you I thought . . . I told you I thought I was falling in love with you."

I'm not sure how to respond to this. It is a statement of vast import. Then again, we are not really having a conversation. Not in the true, face-to-face, tangled-in-history-made-sheets sense of the word. No, owing to pioneering scientific minds (dating back to Alexander Graham Bell), this is a digital simulation of conversation. It isn't real. It is not reality.

I hear her sigh in the silence.

"And now I think that was a mistake," her simulacrum goes on. "I feel like it was wrong of me. Like I was putting pressure on you. I shouldn't have said anything. I'm sorry I said it, because then you felt like you had to say it."

"That's not why I said it." I remind myself that it's not my voice she will hear, only a near-simultaneous reconstruction of it. That reconstructed voice is trembling now, too. "I said it because I meant it." And how could I not "mean it," when "it" was nothing more than proffering a possibility, not even a probability?[12]

"Yeah, but you shouldn't have. Things are going to change. Time goes quicker than you think. We're going to graduate . . . I don't want you to make decisions because of me, okay? Can you promise me that? That when you make your decisions, you'll make them for yourself, not for me?"

I suddenly feel as though I could answer George's *Why?* with a final and definitive *because*. *Because she's good*, I could say to him, *and good at what she does. She's committed. She's varsity-level acting talent, if we ranked such a thing in such a fashion. And she hews to what she wants, but she surrenders what she wants when it's for the greater good. Is that enough?* I would ask George and perhaps others not-George. *Is that good enough?*

"Promise me," she commands.

If this were a real conversation, I don't know if I could make that promise. If she were with me, I might refuse to forsake her or to eschew her dreams and desires in favor of my own. But I cannot see her. I cannot touch her. So I make the promise. After all, it's just a digital copy of a promise; if broken, it can't be as wrong as breaking the real thing.

Later, I try to remember the details of the dream, but they have faded (as dream details do) except for the CLEAN IS MY ANAGRAM badge and the comment that I haven't finished my college apps; I cannot finish them because I don't know "something important." Something about the future? I rise from bed to turn off my desk lamp, but first I straighten the papers on my desk, idly glancing through them, wondering what I am doing . . .

That's when I see it.

There, on the app for College Y. My heart races as I flip through the others—R, H, P, M, D—on every single one, I find the same flaw. Or rather, the same absence; I see what is *not* there, rather than seeing what *is* there. Everything is filled out except for one single piece of information: my last name. My last name is blank in every instance.

I don't know my own last name.

---

12. *I think I'm falling in love with you, too* is meaningless speculation.

iCLOUD HACK SUCCESSFUL!

Downloading contents of iMessage chat between
AUTHOR (Barry Lyga) and EDITOR

BARRY LYGA: OK, I like that you've kept the ending of this chapter, but as we move into Chapter 6, there's no payoff for Mike not knowing his last name. We just move on to the next bit and we don't get around to explaining the whole last name thing until much later.

EDITOR: Barry, it's the same way in the original book.

BARRY LYGA: Never mind.

CHAPTER 6

Phil is right: time moves quickly.

She assembles a senior play, breathtaking in scope, and unites an uninterested student body through sheer Phil-ness, through her ungodly yet godlike willpower. Nothing in the production coheres; she is deliberately casting and designing the play counter to every line on its pages. But it works, because the Phil-ness is contagious; her belief that it can happen infects everyone, making it so that it does/will happen. Designing and building sets for her, I have a literal and figurative backstage pass that enables me to watch her stampede and badger and implore the play into being—as though she were nursing a whole herd of wounded animals not only to life but into a unified pack. It is a *Waiting for Godot* replete with action sequences and elaborate sets. It is contrary to every dream of Samuel Beckett, the play's author. It shouldn't work. It *does* work. The performance is a triumph.

Phil is a triumph. She is gloriously victorious, and better yet, she does not care for the accolades and the bouquets. She cares only for the knowledge that she birthed her vision into the world, whole and unmaimed by the mundane considerations of others. She accepts congratulations, but does not need them. She smiles at acknowledgments of her success, but the inner satisfaction of her success shows only in the glow of her eyes. The approbation of the crowd means little to her, not out of hubris or ego, but rather out of a fierce sense of self-challenge.

She takes my breath away. Then gives it back when we kiss.

As our senior year hurtles toward graduation, she accepts a scholarship offer from the nearby state university, while I stand at a decision nexus among three different colleges, one of which is close enough to home that Phil and I could easily see each other every day—or at least as frequently as we wished. The other two of which are far enough from home as to guarantee that I won't see her until Thanksgiving. Phil asks almost every day if I've arrived at a decision. Denying that I am eager to leap into the world of Y would be false—something she knows, having borne witness to the kitchen table full of admissions material, which led to the sheet-washing, which led to our almost-fight after the dream, which led to . . . here. Her denial that she might be falling in love with me notwithstanding, her behavior suggests that she *is* in love with me.

I am not sure if I am in love with her or not. But I cannot imagine (if this is *not* love) that love (whatever it is) could be any better. True, we have our problems, our "issues," but we still roll around in the sheets, the history now washed clean on a weekly basis with the rest of the laundry; we still steal kisses in the halls between classes at what is still the WB. What more is there? Given all of that, then, how could I even flick an eye in the direction of leaving her? The universe itself seems to have put us together, prompting the inevitable question: Who am I to separate us, even if that means not living my dream and forgoing Y?

"Dude, you're a master of denial," George says to me on the subway to school. "Well, more like a master of self-deception."

"Thanks, man. I'll miss you next year, too."

He rolls his eyes, gripping the subway pole with both hands so he won't go flying into fellow commuters. "Dude, you know what I mean. You've been talking about going to Y since we were kids. It's like your . . . marines, you know what I mean?"

Since before I've known him, George has been obsessed with

enlisting in the marines. Most of us—including his mother—thought it the passing fancy of childhood, the way we all wanted to be astronauts or firefighters or veterinarians as children. George did not so much grow out of his yearning as grow into it, the desire flourishing and thriving as he aged. For him to compare my love of Y to his love of the marines is a potent thing indeed.

"You gotta do it," he went on. "Forget about her."

Funny: Phil says the same thing on a regular basis. "Forget about me."

But she says it with anger. Phil's anger is a lot like Phil's lust: wide-open, vast, brazen, intimidating. I assume that this anger is aimed at me . . . well, actually, at several versions of me. Not merely at the potential future Y-less Mike, but also at the present Mike for putting her in this position—even at the past Mike for having deceived her about my desire to go to Y in the first place. (*Not myself, George. I deceived Phil. So fuck you and your JV psychology.*) Still, no matter what my choice, I will make her hate me in some way.

Her anger I have suffered many times; I can weather it. Her hatred I cannot fathom, because I do not wish to. So maybe I *am* in a little bit of denial. (Apologies for the "fuck you," George. I am glad you cannot hear my thoughts.) She *has* been angrier than usual recently. Is it a first step on a long, tumultuous road to hatred? The anger flares for no reason, or for the absurdly trivial: letting go of her hand "too soon" in the hall, kissing her "too quickly," texting her back "too late." What I so adored about her—that steadfast refusal to mitigate her temper with apology—is becoming increasingly senseless and nonsensical.

I chalk it up to the stress of *Godot*, knowing it's not the case, or at least not the whole case.

So . . . *do* I love her?

As I ponder the question, I notice a kid standing nearby. He's eating an ice cream cone, and it disgusts me. It's morning, right? Too early to be eating ice cream. Even my brother wouldn't eat ice cream this early. The kid looks vaguely familiar, but I shove the thought aside. What do I care about *him*? I care about Phil. Maybe the fact that I'm wondering is in itself my answer. What do I love *about* her? Do I love her naturally blue hair, rich as the ocean depths? Or is that merely a symbol of her ineffable singularity?

Is it her belief in me? Her body arching under mine, bent against mine, hovering above mine? Her otherworldly talent for willing collaborative art into reality? Her strength and belief and commitment? Are those the only "positives?" Or are these questions all pieces of the same puzzle, one I can only solve by trying to be with someone else, if only in order to determine the truth by comparison?

Going to Y, I would have to break up with her. I've learned enough from books and film, from my own *parents*, that no good ever comes of a long-distance relationship. Mom and Dad both attempted to stay with their respective significant others post-college in spite of moving here. After they met, it was all over. I've known this my whole life, but the information suddenly feels new and terrifying, a frigid snake slithering through my rib cage. Who knows the sort of woman I might meet at Y? It has an intensive four-year architecture BA program. *She could be an architect.* This thought, truly idiotic, is less a snake and more a roller-coaster plunge, thrilling and nauseating in spite of (or because of) its idiocy.

Should a comparison ever arise—in a cold analysis—I must admit to Phil's quirks. Or rather, to specific moments of irritation. Like expecting me to deliver those gummi bears when she knew I was with George. Or craving that strange and vaguely creepy bed reading session. Insisting I come to her that rainy night . . . which, in hindsight, could very easily be interpreted as a puerile attempt on her part to interfere with my application process. The truth is that I have cataloged myriad incidents (ranging from bizarre to odd to rude to outright ridiculous) and if I did not *fear* Phil's anger as much as I adore it, I would have fought back.

I understand her anger, which mitigates it somewhat, but not entirely. She is caught in that liminal space between compassion and greed, sensing that my path to happiness does not align with hers, that I must hie me to College Y, while she stays behind. And I? I am caught in a different liminal space, the one between certitude and bemusement. If I leave, I *could* be happy, and Phil *will* be unhappy. If I stay, I *could* be unhappy and Phil . . .

Phil could go either way. Happy that I am here. Angry that I've sacrificed my certain happiness for her potential joy.

I should be confused.

Instead . . . I feel guilty. She knows that I obfuscated Y's importance; worse, she knows that I did *not* obfuscate with my parents or with George or with anyone else. With them, I've been honest about my desire to go to Y. So perhaps she knows what I hadn't known myself until this very moment: I *can't* get as angry as she can. I've never been honest enough with her to legitimize such anger. My guilt is one set of a zipper's teeth, my fear is the other, and together they keep my mouth shut tight.

Maybe George wasn't so far off about me after all.

"Dude, want some?" he asks, wrenching me back to reality.

He waves a protein bar at me. The wrapper is peeled back, banana-like. My insides squeeze, and I snap my head back, recoiling.

"Oh, right," George mutters, pulling it away. "Chocolate. Sorry."

Luckily, I haven't experienced the overwhelming smell of chocolate syrup since the night of the Phil-interrupted dream. But the odor of chocolate still repulses me, and now it reminds me of how I faced the Third Wall again, how I trembled with mounting, ignorant fear when I realized I did not know my own last name.

How could I just go to someone and *ask* for my last name? How could I confess that I did not know this basic, crucial, *assumed* piece of information? I would have checked my driver's license if I'd had one, but I don't. Ultimately, I relied (as always) on George. Sunday morning I took forms to his house and asked him—as a favor, to be repaid by a favor of equal inconvenience at any time—to please correct any errors or fill out any information that was missing because I'd "been staring at them too long to see any dumb mistakes I might have made." I didn't specify that I was unaware of my own last name. George merely shrugged and flipped through the pages, and then with a smirk he went online and typed my last name in each blank. I avoided watching as he did so, convinced beyond any sense of logic that if I had gone this long without knowing my last name, I could and can—and, perhaps, must—go longer.

The distraction and the memory, precipitated by George's accidental offer of hated chocolate, have cleared my mind. And as the subway sways and reels along on its tracks, the train of my thoughts reels and rolls before finding stability on its own set of psychological tracks . . . and the first passenger to enter the open doors of this hackneyed metaphorical train is not Phil; it is College Y, and that tells me everything I need to know.

CHAPTER 7

Phil could also be wrong.

Time is thick—a sludge; we move through it one heartbeat at a time.

Time is thin—it's paper; a page turned, and the world changes.

Time is on the event horizon of a black hole—everything happens at once, always and forever. It passes neither quickly nor slowly. The past and the future are the present, and the present is the present, too.

I'm sitting at the edge of my narrow little bed in my dorm room, looking at a text.

It's spring break of my freshman year, and I have decided to stay at College Y instead of going home or embarking on a drunken road trip with my bros (of which I have none)—but more to the point, my first major architecture project is due . . . and while the relative silence is conducive to intense focus on my work, denial can only go so far; I've been alone for three days now, festering in my own loser-dom.

As I stare at my cell phone, I'm transported to the day Phil and I stripped her bed; everything changed that day. It's so clear now. But I was able to convince myself that we were carrying on as before, just on laundered sheets.

The text reads:

can i use your shower?

Five words and one punctuation mark on the screen. My body freezes; my mind races backward and forward again. I have not seen Phil since August. It was the natural conclusion to a trend; during the last weeks of senior year, post–*Waiting for Godot*, we saw each other less and less. We were no longer "together," but we did not yet know how to be "apart." Summer brought freedom from Phil and secret relief, and likewise no doubt it brought Phil the same. Yet without her I plummeted into an odd sort of null-emotional hole—the abyss I'd first glimpsed, teetering at the precipice, while staring at the sheets in a rumpled heap on the floor of her room. But even if I *were* a master of self-delusion, I still had drive. College Y–bound, I buried myself in preparation for that hallowed (clichéd) rite of passage, Boy Leaves Home. I spent more time with my parents and my brother. I hung out with George as much as possible before he shipped out for basic training. While I yearned for Phil, for her body against mine, I denied to the world/myself that I missed her.

Two weeks before I left town, we bumped into each other— literally—rounding the same corner at the local Staples as we each loaded up on last-minute supplies, acting on a neurotic impulse of most incoming first-year college students. After the initial "whoa"-ing and "hey"-ing and "oh my God it's you"-ing and the bursts of nervous laughter, we shared an empty "How have you been?" Followed by, "Fine. Busy!" The encounter lasted thirty seconds at most—an accidental moment of physical contact that somehow served to extinguish any further contact whatsoever.

And then (now, rather), this random request to use my shower.

"I'm in town for a show," she answers when I call.

No hello, even. She's skipping the formalities. (*How have you been for the past nine months, and what is College Y like?*) But I smile, feeling a pang for the Phil I once pined for, the one who dispensed with all bullshit in favor of getting to the point.

"Mike? You there?"

"Yeah. I mean . . . I'm here. I'm not home, though—"

"I know, I know. Your brother told me," she interrupts, talking fast, preventing me from asking her how, when, and why she talked to my brother about my spring break schedule. "We're staying with the lead's sister, but she only has one shower. I don't feel like standing in line to take a cold shower. I can borrow a car and come over. I promise I won't be long."

I consider lying. I imagine telling her that I am busy with an imaginary human being, for no other reason than shame. Didn't I come here in part on the promise (premise?) of "meeting someone new" at Y, a special Y-woman who would out-Phil Phil, a Y-woman absent any annoying negatives? And yet here I am, Phil-less, Phil-replacement-less—and let's face it, friendless. I've made no friends at all at Y. I have casual acquaintances. Worse is that in my darkest, loneliest, most honest moments, I have to admit that my judgment of Phil's "negatives" is, in retrospect, pathetic (on my part, not hers). Her major crime? Above all others? Reaching out to me. And for that, I excommunicated her, cast her aside, avoided emails and phone calls. Was this all a wrong decision? Coming to Y may have been the right decision, but was breaking up with Phil the wrong one? Could we have survived the "long-distance" thing? (My parents are frequently wrong about almost everything, as parents are.) Moreover . . . could we still?

As these thoughts/questions swirl, I hear myself say, "Sure."

"Okay. Thanks. I'll be over in a little while." She hangs up before either of us can say another word.

When the knock at the door comes, I am unprepared, even though I have done nothing *but* prepare myself. For twenty minutes I've fretted in the bathroom mirror, scrutinizing every hair and blemish while simultaneously reliving memories of my roommates' sexual exploits—having experienced them either in real time (the suite walls are paper thin; more than once I've worn noise-canceling headphones in order to sleep) or the morning after, thanks to explicit boast-fests I would find grotesque even if I were getting any action myself. But I am not. It is easy to see why. The Mike who bumped into Phil last summer has been replaced by this sad-sack reflection—flabbier, paler, more haggard . . . a fetid cheese of an ex-boyfriend past his prime.[13]

Phil is the same Phil, and yet she's new all at once, wearing jeans I've never seen before, a T-shirt with the State mascot on it, a green wind-breaker. Her hair, still that lustrous blue, is shorter now. Even her posture has changed; the way she slouches in the doorway, a knapsack slung over her left shoulder, casts a subtle light on something new and fiery, almost cocky. She has metamorphosed in the caesura of our companionship, in ways so small (that domino-fall into larger changes) that the specifics are unknowable, their existence unavoidable. What has she become? And how?

She lunges forward and hugs me before speaking.

"It's good to see you," she finally murmurs, stepping away. "How've you been?"

"Fine," I tell her. I'm not sure it's a lie, but I am certain that it isn't the truth, either.

Stepping inside, she takes a moment to survey the squalor: the filthy couch, the discarded laundry, a half-eaten bag of pretzels on the floor. Eventually, her eyes come to rest on the "coffee table" (so quoted because it is in fact a discarded public restroom door, origins unknown, propped up on cinder blocks). She nods toward what sits upon it, a poster-board architectural model-in-progress, a strip mall powered by solar panels and a windmill.

"What's that?" she asks.

"One of my assignments. We have to convert a former church lot into retail space."

"Nice. That's symbolic, I guess."

"I . . . guess?" I actually hadn't thought about it.

"Sort of a commentary on contemporary mores and society, right?"

---

13. This excellent sentence was written not by the Author, but rather by the Editor. Which (pun incoming) cheeses off the Author quite a bit.

"Um, it's just an assignment. It wasn't my idea."

"Well, you made it green, at least."

It takes me a second to realize she isn't talking about the model's color. The poster board is bone white. She's talking about my hypothetical strip mall's energy source, its environmental soundness—not my idea, either. Suddenly I feel moronic, unworthy of college-level chitchat.[14]

"I'm sure you'll kick ass," she adds. "You always do. Speaking of ass-kicking, how's George doing in the marines?"

"Uh, fine. He . . . I don't get to talk to him a lot, but the last time he seemed good."

Silence falls between us.

"So, where's the shower?" she asks, slinging her knapsack off her back. "Don't worry. I brought my own towel."

"Oh, right. I mean, good."

I quickly show her to the bathroom. Only when I hear the faucet turn and the water running do I allow myself to breathe and think, *She brought her own towel.* Given the general state of filth here, that was wise. But I wasn't worried about it. I'd completely forgotten why she'd come here in the first place. Seeing Phil again is affecting me more deeply than I would have or could have imagined. Does she want me back? Is she really even in town for a show? What show? Why has she given me no details? Where is she staying? Would her hosts really have run out of hot water? The questions squirm and writhe in my brain, reproducing exponentially, a host of fertilized embryonic cells . . . until I hear the telltale squeak of the water being turned off.

Moments later, Phil emerges from the bathroom. She's clad only in a towel—as pristine and white as the model of my hypothetical strip mall. The questions evaporate. I'm left only with thoughts of what lies beneath that towel. I remind myself not to stare.

"What show are you doing?" I blurt out.

"Can we talk about it later?" she asks quietly, avoiding my eyes. "I'm

---

14. Another instance of the Editor adding something subtly excellent to the story. Perhaps the whole thing would be better off without an Author at all.

tired. This is the first time I've been able to relax. The sleeping arrangements on this trip aren't ideal, either." She looks up. "Actually, can I lie down on your bed? Just a quick nap, I promise. A power nap."

How can I deny her that? I point toward my bedroom. She steps inside and does not so much close the door as bring it *close* to being closed. The fact that it remains open a crack seems like an invitation, making me think of a corny old joke my parents used to tell me: Q: When is a door not a door? A: When it's ajar! Or, I suppose, when it is an invitation . . . ha, ha, ha. Thinking of my parents makes me think of long-distance relationships. I want to think of neither of those things right now. So I stop thinking. I slip into the room, into the bed, et cetera.

The towel already lies in a heap on the floor.

It's perfect. It's like old times. It's been so long.

"It's been so long," Phil says, slipping her arms around my waist.

"Yes," I say.

"Did you think about this?" she asks.

"Yes."

"How? How did you think about it?"

Her voice, clotted with lust and satisfaction.

And mine, useless and weak: "Um . . ."

When it's all over, Phil exercises an admirable and peculiar ability of hers. She drops off into a deep sleep without hesitation or pause. So she really *was* tired. Which means she was telling the truth? (About needing a power nap?) Now that she's snoring, the questions tumble back into my brain—less a growing promise of new life, more a heap of dirty laundry dumped into a swirling spin cycle. I slide back from her, as far as the narrow twin college bed will allow. I stretch these new history-made sheets tight. *Is* this new history, the beginning of a new timeline? Or is this post-history? Nostalgia sex? (Or as she might say, "One last time, with feeling"? Her go-to exhortation during the final *Godot* rehearsals.) Maybe this is some new and as yet unidentified relationship. Maybe now we're long-distance friends with benefits.

I collapse back and stare up at the ceiling.

Before I know it, I'm falling asleep, too. And I start to dream, though this time I am aware I'm dreaming from the start. I am conscious of a narrative that makes no sense and has no discernible beginning . . .

I'm in a laundromat. A woman stands in front of me, blocking my path to the dryer. Her hair is black, glistening like wet coal. I have no idea how old she is. Anywhere between eighteen and forty-five.

"Once my hair was blond," she says to me. "And then I was pushed."

"I thought there were no quotation marks in dreams," I reply. Odd that I am aware of quotation marks and at the same time aware of my wondering—aware of awareness.

"Of course there are quotation marks in dreams," she says. Imagine how complicated it would be without them, she says or does not say.

"Cool," I reply in my dream state, wondering if this is what drugs are like.

"My name is Angia. Angia Eiphon. Does that name mean anything to you?"

It doesn't, but I know it should, because it's familiar. Something tickles at the back of my mind: An allegory. Or a metaphor. Or a riddle. *Clean is my anagram.*

"Mike loved me," she continues. "And God loved me. But then God pushed me and I fell so far, out of dreams, into the world—"

"Where did you go?" I interrupt. I feel a sudden urgency (fear, even) that Phil will wake me up again. I can hear the sound of snoring. "Where did you land?"

"Somewhere else. Somewhere unreal and real at the same time."

"Am I supposed to know who you are?"

"I don't know what you're supposed to know. I'm the sister of the first Mike. And his lover."

"Oh. Gross."

The urgency (fear) passes. I try to peer past Angia Eiphon at the dryer, to see if it's stopped spinning.

"No, no. It's not like that, not straight-up incest. It's complicated."

"Yeah, sounds like it—"

"Mike, pay attention to me, okay? You ever try to get a chocolate syrup stain out of a sheet?" Now she has my attention. The urgency (fear) is back. *Chocolate syrup?* "Good, no quotes," Angia Eiphon says. "So you're listening. I don't know why I'm here in your dream. It might be a delaying tactic. Or flat-out desperation: God's convenient excuse to move things along, to allow time to pass until God figures out what God is trying to do. Which, by the way, may never happen."

I stare into her eyes, as black and shiny and sphinxlike as her alleged former blond hair. "What are you talking about?"

"If I knew that, I'd tell you, too. How about this: I'll tell you something else instead. I'll tell you to wake up right now. And you will."

"No! I mean, wait. Please. Just—"

"Wake up."

Phil is already awake. That's the first thing I notice. (Well, that and that I've bolted upright in a cold sweat.) She has also changed clothing; she's wearing a dress now, a strappy black dress I've never seen before. But of course she has changed; she came to take a shower, so why would she put back on dirty clothes? I open my mouth to speak, and I can't, because each possible utterance is pregnant with the potential to create a new universe of unanswerable questions—no, multiple universes; no, infinite universes, in turn spinning off into infinite possibilities . . .

I love you, Phil, or—

This was a mistake, Phil, or—

Did you really just come here for a shower? or—

Are you seeing anyone? or—

Does this mean we're back together? or even—

What the hell, Phil?

The problem is that I do not want to live in any one of those universes. I want to live (rather, I need to live) in all of them simultaneously. I must know the answers to every question, as well as the many others I have not listed—so that with those answers I can know the next question(s) to ask, and so on and so forth, until I can arrive at the final, right conclusion. How can I know what I think of what has just happened until I know why it has happened?

"Thanks for the shower," Phil says.

"Are you leaving?"

"Yeah." She lets out a puzzled laugh. "I told you I wouldn't be long."

And she did tell me that. In those exact words. But that was before she slid, shower-soft, into my bed, before we began a new history on sheets laundered, conveniently and coincidentally enough, this very morning, meaning . . . what? Who would insist that she honor a pledge made in one universe now that she lives in another? Did she even make such a pledge? Or did I just wish it into existence?

"We should stay in touch," says Phil, pulling on her windbreaker. She pauses at the door. "I miss talking to you."

Talking to me, I ponder, once she's left. *Talking* to me. She misses *talking* to me. Talking! I don't miss talking to me at all. Talking to me is all I have right now.

iCLOUD HACK SUCCESSFUL!

Downloading contents of email from
Barry Lyga's account . . .

FROM: Barry Lyga

TO: *** *********

SUBJECT: Goddamnit!

"Talking to me is all I have right now."

Damn it, ***! That wasn't in the original manuscript. You added it and it's PERFECT and now I'm so angry that I didn't think of it. Is it a cop-out for me to add it to *Unedited*? It's so great! Shit, I'm so angry!!!

CHAPTER 8

After spring break, with the end of freshman year hurtling toward summer, I finally take up my roommates on their offer to "take [me] out and get [me] some strange [offensive word here]."

They mean to introduce me to a girl who will make me forget about Phil; more to the point, they succeed, if only for a sludgy-fast moment in time.

One Saturday night, before final exams, I am dragged to a party and thrown in front of a petite blond premed student, a friend of two of my roommates' current girlfriends. ("She told us she thinks you're cute, Mike!") Fueled by alcohol,[15] I experience a flash of hope that Phil is behind me, at least figuratively. The truth? I remember little other than my own attempts to stifle the delighted bullying/encouragement from my roommates[16] . . . a haze of giggly/angry responses: middle finger raised in a toast to their raised bottles; a surreptitious thumbs-down to a gleeful thumbs-up; a mouthed *Fuck you* to a hooted "You dog!" In the end, the petite blond premed captures my attention by doing the

15. Mike rarely gets drunk, another factor that distinguishes him and isolates him from his roommates. (Peeing in the suite toilet with consistent accuracy is another.) Often he wonders how they got into College Y in the first place, even whether if indeed College Y is truly the sacred temple of intellectual pursuit it presents itself to be, but he knows that their families are wealthier than his. It might be that simple.

16. And their girlfriends.

exact opposite of our facilitators: she purposely and purposefully ignores them. She ignores everything but *me*, and when I can focus long enough to reciprocate, I discover (fuzzily) that she is funny, interesting, attractive . . . and, yes, willing.

We end up in her room, in her bed, et cetera. After all that, my last clear memory/image is of Phil.

Phil has sprung to mind, and I can't dislodge her, no matter how hard I try.

Very well, I console myself as the premed student sleeps beside me. I wonder how long I should wait before slipping away into the night. *Very well, so I thought of Phil while in bed with someone else—only the second "someone else" in my life. It is probably natural to think of Phil the first time I sleep with someone not-Phil, right? And on the plus side, I have no desire to get drunk again anytime soon,* for which I suppose I owe all parties concerned in this brief anecdote a debt of thanks.

Very well.

Weeks pass with no word from Phil. If she misses talking to me, she is not interested in finding a solution to this problem. At least not now.

Interesting how time works: when the shame-filled avoidance of the petite premed blond reaches a mutual boiling point with my shameful longing to talk to Phil—my life reduced to a confluence of awfulness—I receive the following email:

Mike,

I'm not sure how to tell you, so I'm just going to tell you: I've gotten back together with [him]. I didn't want to tell you before because I know how stressed you've been with school and everything, and I didn't want to add to that burden. A part of me sort of hates you, but a part of me also hates me, too, so in a weird way, I think that makes us even. Maybe?

I really believe in you. It's important to me that you know that. I think you're going to have such an amazing life and achieve your dreams and build some truly magnificent things, buildings and structures like no one else has ever imagined. And I believe that after some time, I'll stop hating you and I'll stop hating myself and we can really be friends again, which I would like.

You don't have to answer. I totally understand if you hate me right now.

Phil

I write, almost immediately:

Phil,

Thanks for letting me know. I'm happy for you.

A lie (I think).

And I don't hate you.

(I think.)

I don't want you to hate yourself, either. I hope you're happy and that when you feel up to it, you'll get in touch with me and we can be friends.

Mike

It almost does not matter if I send the email or not. In physics class, I have learned of the wave-particle duality of light. The theory supposes that light, which anecdotally and evidentially exhibits the properties of both wave and particle, *is in fact both at once*. But in order to understand its nature, it must collapse into one or the other category, depending upon the circumstances . . . and most crucially, upon the observer. My relationship with Phil has now similarly collapsed. Potentially romantic and not-romantic at the same time, it—now observed—stands as nonromantic: a reality made real by my observation.

She's back with *him*. It's over.

I click Send.

I call George. He still believes he is my best friend, and will always believe. "Man, I made a mistake," I tell him.

"Dude," says George.[17] "You have to remember the shit about her that drove you crazy."

"That's what I'm remembering."

"I don't mean the *good* crazy. I mean the bad crazy, you know what I mean?"

"That stuff just doesn't seem so bad anymore, is all."

"Dude. Please. You been getting laid up there?"

"I thought about Phil the whole time. What does that have to do with anything?"

"You're lonely. You don't have anyone else, so you miss Phil."

"Didn't you hear me? I was with someone. I was with someone and I thought about Phil the whole time."

"How long's it been since she told you?"

"Three days."

"What have you been doing?"

"Nothing."

"You mean that literally, don't you? You haven't done anything."

My room is a litter of unfinished work, unread books, unlaundered clothing, uneaten boxes of store-brand doughnuts. It is as though time has hiccuped—I can remember nothing of the intervening days between the email and this phone call. Surely I've eaten? The evidence

---

17. Per military rules, George's cell was confiscated during training; he returns my call from a pay phone on Parris Island.

is all around me, but I don't recall any specifics. Surely I've showered? Changed? Peed?[18] Slept?

"I should have said something when she was here." I am dodging. "At spring break. I should have said something to her."

"Why didn't you?"

"I don't know." But I do: I was, at the time, under the mistaken impression that I did not love Phil. "I should have told her I loved her. That would have changed things."

"Dude, you don't know that. For all you know, she was already back with *him* when she came to see you."

"I don't believe that. That's not like her. She wouldn't do that. Why would she do that?"

"Who knows? She's a person. People are complicated. What are you doing?"

"You mean right now? Nothing. Talking to you."

"Me, too. I'm not doing anything. Just talking to you, you know what I mean?"

"Okay."

"Dude, you need to chill out, okay? I can hear you stressing all the way down here, and I'm in fucking boot camp. It's no good. You're done with her now."

"No. No, I'm not. She was with *him* before and she picked me. It can happen again."

"Dude."

"I made it happen once before. I can do it again. She doesn't love *him*. She never said she loved *him*."

"Did she ever say she loved *you*?"

"Sort of."[19]

"Dude."

"I have to tell her. I have to tell her I love her. That will change everything."

---

18. It was "pissed" in the original. I just thought you should know that.
19. *"Do you want to hear something scary?" Phil asks.*

"Dude, don't do this to yourself. Move on."

"But I can fix it, George! Don't you get it?"

"You can't fix anything. There's nothing *to* fix. When does your semester end?"

"Less than a month. I'll be back home on the fifteenth."

"I'll call you when you get home, okay? I should be able to call then. Try not to lose your mind before then."

"Okay."

He hangs up. Only then do I realize that I never asked him about boot camp—further proof (if any were needed) that I am *not* his best friend.

After that, I call Phil.

I hit End before the phone can ring once. Because . . . am I sure I am in love with Phil? I can't imagine how I am *not* in love with Phil. Have I not missed her, yearned for her almost from the beginning? Did I not bed her without hesitation when offered the opportunity? Have I not spent the weeks since—even with the blond petite premed—in lusting misery? Have I not, since the revelation of her resumption of relations with *him*, fallen into a useless daze, barely feeding myself, barely able to rouse myself to use the bathroom for its intended purpose, unshaven, unshowered? What else could these signs be, if not symptoms of all-consuming love?

By process of elimination, there is no other possibility.

Without thought or artifice or construction, I know that I love Phil.

The second time I call her, her phone rings, committing me.

Hanging up now would accomplish nothing—my name and number would linger on her missed calls list, fingerprints of my intention. On the second ring, alarm creeps into my heart like a cat with distemper. Has she seen the caller ID and chosen not to answer? Worse, is she with *him*? Right now? The third ring harkens impending voicemail. What would I say? I would have to say *some*thing, wouldn't I? I couldn't simply leave the mute evidence of an entry in missed calls, with so much unspoken and easily misimagined on Phil's part. I would have to say something to her voicemail, but a blurted protestation of love could not be that something.

Fourth and final ring—

"Hey," she answers, as casual as any "hey" she ever offered when we were a couple, neither warm nor cold.

"Hey," I say back.

"What's up?" she asks without inflection. (Translation: *I'm alone and available to talk*. Or possibly: *I'm not alone, but spit it out, chump*. There's really no way to tell which.) I feel foolish for bothering her, for interrupting whatever she was doing—with or without *him*.

"I just wanted to tell you something, is all."

"Okay."

"I know I screwed up. I know I messed things up. But . . ."

"Yeah?"

"I love you."

There's no pause before her answer, no hesitation, no intervention bridging to the now. "I don't love you. I'm sorry."

She does not sound sorry. She sounds both agitated and bored at the same time. Perhaps, I think, she *is* agitated and bored at this moment.

"It's okay," I say, absolving her for I know not what, for reasons I know not why, save that when people apologize, I tell them it's okay.

"Mike," she says after a moment. "Mike. You can't—"

"Don't."

"You can't just . . . Look, you're going to meet someone else." (The tears start. Mine, not hers. My first tears since childhood.) "Someone really great," she finishes. Her tone is the same comforting, casual, confidential Phil tone I've known all along—possessing its own special gravity, weighty enough to flatten me.

Then silence.

Then, "Are you crying?"

If I admit the truth, would that change her mind? Could my tears prove to her what my words have not, transmitting my love as though through osmosis?

"No," I lie, wiping tears from my cheek. "I'm fine. I just wanted to tell you." Then I add, "I'll talk to you later."

If I had a reason for doing this, if such reasons existed at all, they would make no sense to me. Why would I talk to her later? Why would I talk to her at all? What is there at all to say? By "later," does she think I mean I'll call her later in the day? What am I doing?

"I want us to be friends, Mike," she tells me, sounding like a therapist. "Soon."

In response, apparently no longer capable of speech, I sniffle.

"Okay," she says. "Have a good rest of the semester."

"You, too," I croak automatically.

And then she's gone, and I hold the cell in my hand for a long time, as if it is the hand of a recently deceased loved one—apropos, as I am, both literally and figuratively, *unable to let go*. I clutch that phone/hand as though by so doing I could wrest that same loved one back from death, out of Charon's grasp, out of the gondola of death and back to the living shore of the River Styx . . . Enough. I throw it onto my bed and run to the bathroom, suddenly worried I might barf. In doing so I catch sight of myself in the mirror, and instead of barfing I weep loudly and unashamedly—no telephone, no Phil to deceive, no roommates to impress. I cry, I cry, I cry, watching the tears run down my face, watching the rims of my eyes grow redder and more swollen, and I speak at last to the Mike in the mirror, maybe the me whose grief is precisely and reversely mine . . . and what do I tell him?

Do I tell him the obvious? That what he's done is both grotesque and wrong? That he treated Phil like a thing, not a person, like a prize to be won, and that no matter how glorious and cherished and beloved a prize may be, it is still merely a prize?

What *do* I tell him?

For the first time ever, the truth.

"You deserve this," I tell him. "This is what you deserve."

There is, I discover, a strange sort of desperation that comes from the aftermath of carrying a full complement of Love (capital *L*) with nowhere to set it down. That sort of Love, like caffeine, makes you jittery and nervous. That sort of Love compels you to a strange cycle of action/inaction. I spend hours reloading my email and double-, triple-, and quadruple-checking my cell phone for texts. I also spend hours doing nothing at all, lying on my bed, staring up at the ceiling as though answers had been inscribed there long ago. If life were magically realistic, perhaps those answers would reveal themselves through the paint. But my life is not that way.

My life feels Shakespearean (with all of the profundity and pretentiousness that implies, another unfortunate byproduct of capital-*L* Love): written by an idiot, full of sound and fury, signifying nothing. Therefore I am both ashamed and not-ashamed to confess that frequently I cry, that occasionally I think I might die, and that daily I think I see her . . . anywhere and everywhere. (She came to College Y once, didn't she? Couldn't she come again?) Every time I close my eyes, she's there again. And when I sleep. When I *can* sleep.

She could be full of regret.

She could be yearning for me right now, waiting for me to call, not calling me herself, as she is convinced that I am heartbroken . . . as she is.

She could be *afraid* to call me.

Sometimes (frequently) this particular delusion reaches a fever pitch, and I pick up the phone to call. But I never go through with it because she might be with *him*. I am convinced that she was with *him* both when she wrote the email and received my first call. She's *waiting* for me to make the real call, to set things straight. I stare at the cell. She said, "I'm *with* someone else." That's all she said. There are entire universes between "love" and "with." We "love" parents, siblings, children, pets, spouses. We are "with" strangers on a bus, on a subway, in a movie theater, at the grocery store. Phil is "with" *him*, but she love(d/s) me.

She communicated that love in covert words and phrases, in questions and indirections that I never decoded because Phil never seemed to need decoding. And I didn't see it until now, until distance and time forced me to reexamine every instance of our relationship, parse every word spoken, dissect her in a savage hunt for hope. *Phil. Oh, Phil. Oh, beautiful, blue-tressed Phil . . .* I speak to you in a dream that needs no quotation marks, because you dominate the waking nightmare of my real life.

But what if I'm wrong? What if I've misinterpreted my own memories?

Memories are, after all, subjective. There's no official record outside my tortured brain. I can't scour the facts by flipping back through the page of some objective tome, inscribed in such a way that the truth would be set apart—a poster-board model of a strip mall: the lone shining item in an environment defined by filth, the lone symbol of clarity and possibility.

I could be wrong.

I could also be right.

I don't call her. I'll call her later.

At the end of the year, my architecture professor summons me for reasons unknown, wanting to see my sketchbook. I slink into his office and flop into a leather-backed chair, facing him across his wide drafting table—slouching like a child sent to the principal's office, unsure as to precisely what sin I have committed.

I hate and respect and envy him. He loves to teach. He is passionate about buildings and cityscapes and urban planning. He takes leaves of absence when hired to design interesting projects. I seek his approval. He looks the way I want to look when I am his age: no beard, no tattoos, no piercings.

He smiles from behind his desk, not looking up as he bids me to close the door and waves me into the seat. Then he laughs, realizing that I am already sitting. "Mike, you are one of the most promising . . ." He leaves the sentence hanging and gestures for my sketchbook.

I shove it into his hand.

"Ah, thank you. Yes." He flips through the pages, shaking his head. "I like it when students have ambition, but there's a thin line between ambition and overreaching. Are you serious about this final project idea? Building a hotel underwater? Under a transparent dome?"

"It's meant to be reminiscent of an air bubble underwater," I tell him. "To distinguish it from the underwater homes in Dubai. The idea is that you can go down there and see the fish and the wildlife and—"

"The ocean's a big place," he interrupts. "How do you know you'll be near anything at all? What are the odds some fish will just swim by this place?"

Site and context. "I'll put it near a coral reef," I tell him, as though I've planned to do so all along, the thought having just occurred to me, along with the idea that—perhaps—I need to become scuba-trained in order to work on this project. To see the site. The context. To experience it personally, like every good architect should.

"Why a dome?" he asks.

"The dome is as old as Hadrian. Makes you feel like you're under a protective sky."

"But in this case, the occupant is *not* under a protective sky. He's underwater."

"The dome is the best way to manufacture it. Build it on the surface, prefab, and sink it. The dome's structure will diffuse the water pressure from outside. So I can use a thinner acrylic that way. It'll be cheaper."

He shakes his head. "You'll use less acrylic, but manufacturing a curvature means a more expensive building process, so there go your savings. Also, you'll get distortion where the acrylic curves. No one will be able to see there. You need to make a box, not a dome. It's all about refraction. You'll have to invent a whole new science of statics."

Maybe I also need a degree in physics. "But the air-bubble motif—"

"So you'd be better off prefabbing a traditional series of walls"—here, he turns to a blank page in my sketchbook and scratches out four boring walls with efficient pencil strokes—"that have large picture windows of acrylic. Then"—still drawing, each movement of his pencil a violation—"a traditional ceiling, spotted over the bed area with an acrylic porthole of some sort to allow a line of sight to the fish or what have you."

"But that's not the idea. That's just a room underwater. The idea is complete, three-hundred-and-sixty-degree horizontal visibility and a hundred-and-eighty-degree vertical—"

"With no ornamentation or details on the walls? Who do you think you are—Loos?" he jokes.[20]

20. Adolf Loos believed that modern architecture should lack ornamentation, likening ornamentation to tattoos on "savages."

"Only the room would be underwater. The rest of the hotel—reception and all that—would be above water and would look like a normal hotel."

"No one could afford this. You'd have to invent a whole new way of getting electricity and plumbing in there. What about privacy on the inside? Bathroom walls?" I have no answer ready for that, and before I can begin to invent one, he keeps firing at me: "What about something as simple as flushing a toilet under the ocean?"

"A pressurized toilet?" I offer weakly.

"The expense for this thing is massive. Who would build it?"

Now I feel that I am underwater, drowning, panicking for a way out. "Frank Lloyd Wright said that architecture should benefit the end user, not the landlord—"

"Thank you for repeating my lecture back to me," he says sardonically. "I'm flattered. But if no one will build it, it won't benefit anyone."

His tone is so smug and so dismissive that I cannot help but to sit up straight, my own defensiveness commingling with Phil's unadulterated glee at the idea of the underwater hotel.

"Diller and Scofidio. The Blur Building. If they can build an inhabitable cloud, why can't I build an inhabitable air bubble? Wright reinvented the idea of a museum with the Guggenheim. Why can't I reinvent the idea of the hotel?"

He taps the eraser end of his pencil on the table. *One. Two. Three. Tap. Tap. Tap.* "I don't know quite how to break this to you," he says, his tone communicating that he knows precisely how to break it to me, "but you're not Diller and Scofidio. Or Frank Lloyd Wright."

"How do you know that? Maybe I am." It's not really me saying that; it's Phil. Every time someone—usually a teacher or administrator—would tell her she was out of her depth with one of her productions (a female Estragon in a neomodern *Godot*! Othello as a woman! And so on . . .), she would respond to their claims of "You're not ready for this" with . . .

Well, see above.

And now I expect a sigh, or worse. Instead, he chuckles, flips back a few pages in the sketchbook, and again makes a series of pencil strokes there.

"Mike, I like your energy and your imagination. I really do. I don't want to discourage you. But architecture is about marrying the creative and the practical. Be patient. Because . . . I loved your strip mall. That was wonderful." He leans forward, as though telling me a secret, even though there is no one else in the office to overhear. "Sometimes our ambition extends beyond our capabilities. Sometimes we're better off realizing our own limitations. Architecture is an old man's game. Your time will come. In the meantime, focus on the fundamentals and maybe someday you'll get to do something like this."

He slides the sketchbook back to me across the desk.

"I want to do it now," I mutter, snatching the book and cradling it like a frightened child. "Why should I have to wait?"

Scurrying out of his office, I think of Phil's reaction when I first told her about the idea, lying intertwined with me on a library sofa one day, at a time remembered forward in a flashback.

"It's not really practical," I said.

The irony sickens me, my unwitting past echoing my future/present architecture professor.

"Who cares?" she said. "It's cool. It's fun. It's new. I love it. You have to build it someday, and I'll live there with you. It's like living underwater."

I'll live there with you.

Permanence. A promise of some sort of lasting connection. *I'll live there with you.* Belief in me, belief in us, a vow to be together.

I had it. In that moment, I had it and I did not recognize it, and I lost it.

Lost, now.

Phil.

She is memories and regrets now.

I love her, but that love is useless, without purpose. In Alaska, there is a forest of black spruce that stretches for miles along the rail line, wending through the landscape and along the highway, a forest that is dead. An earthquake wrenched the land from its bed and saltwater sluiced inland from the sea, saturating the trees from the roots up so quickly that they were killed and preserved instantly. Traingoers see only a stark forest of still-standing spruce, black as their name. They are like my love—a dead, useless thing, preserved but without life or function or meaning.

Back in my grim little room in my grim little suite, I open the sketchbook.

On the same page featuring the design that so inspired and thrilled Phil, my professor has written TAKE YOUR TIME in neat block letters.

CHAPTER 9

George does not call me when I arrive home for the summer as he promised. Rather, on my second night home, he knocks at my door.

"Dude, I'm not a marine anymore," he says.

I gape at him.

My mind is awhirl. First (again, sad proof of our unequal dynamic in the best-friend department) I think of Phil. She must know that I've come home for the summer, but she has neither called nor texted. Neither has she emailed, nor hailed me on chat. The latter is especially significant because I saw her screen name in my buddy list—meaning she saw mine, too—but did not "hello!" me or acknowledge my cyberexistence. She is so close to me now, only four subway stops away as we reckon city distances. At school, I could forget her for whole minutes at a time, but now her proximity taunts me.

"Don't ask," he adds before clasping my hand and pulling me in for a hug.

Yesterday, when I arrived home, Mom and Dad hugged me, too. The hugs were parental, wistful, lingering. Perhaps their feelings were informed by nostalgia for my youth, now lost to college. My brother did not engage in physical contact, so I slyly offered him a fist, which he shyly bumped with his own. My parents laughed at that, and my brother laughed, and I managed a smile. But I could not laugh, and now my parents know something is wrong, although they also know enough not to smother me with concern.

At the moment, however, I am feeling smothered; George has grown profoundly muscle-bound, and he seems unaware of his new strength.

"What happened?" I blurt out, stepping away. "Sorry. Never mind. Sorry."

"We'll get to that. I've been worried about you, you know what I mean?"

He has been worried about *me*.

Transforming himself into an action hero, humping fifty-pound packs through the heat and humidity of Parris Island, George has been worried about me—while I, for my part, have been worried about . . . me, once again proving that George is my best friend and I am not his.

"I'm okay," I lie with shame and pride, and follow it with "except for" . . . at which point I launch into a litany of confusions and misunderstandings and emotions and recriminations and second guesses: a truly bewildering array of words, nonsequential and nonsensical.

"Dude," George says some time later, "you're a mess."

We're sitting outside. Now that the sun's gone down, the summer desert heat is bearable. I've asked him every question I've asked myself over the past two months, asked him every question I've wanted to ask Phil, then followed those questions with all the same anger, rage, disappointment, sorrow, misery, despondence, and helplessness I've directed at myself . . . how I'd had her and I lost her. Worse yet, threw her away after a second chance.

"I know. But I love her, George. I love her so much."

"This isn't healthy. You've been bottling this stuff up for how long? Months? There was no one to talk to at College Y?"

"Not like this. Not where I could just pour it all out, you know?"

"Dude, you need a change of scenery. Trapped up there all this time. And being back home isn't any good, because you go in that old bedroom and all you can think about is the past." He puts a hand on my shoulder and looks up at the clear, star-speckled sky. "Trust me on that one."

"I just want her back."

"Yeah, I get that. But you don't get to have her back."

"Why not? It's like . . . It's like I feel like there's something I can say or do, some perfect sentence or perfect action that will make her remember that she loves me and—"

"Dude."

"No. Don't stop me. Look, she never said she's in love with *him*. She never said that. Don't you see? She came to me at spring break. *She* came to *me*. That was like a sign, right? Only I didn't get it. But it was just a couple of weeks later that she was with *him*. She gave up on me because I didn't do anything. So now I have to do something."

"You did do something. You told her you love her. And she shot you down."

"She was surprised. She wasn't expecting me to call, to say that. That's all—"

"Then why didn't she call back?"

"Because she knows she hurt me."

I realize, to my own surprise, that I am again crying openly, in front of George. And it's okay. George has just put an arm around me and pulled me close, his small yet strong frame seeming to dwarf my larger one.

"Right. She hurt you. Why would you want to be back with her? She *hurt* you, dude."

"I hurt her, too. So we're even."

I feel him shake his head above my own. "Dude, you said you loved her, and she didn't even hesitate. She just blew you off. Bam. Done. You don't want to be with that person."

But I do. "But I do," I tell him. "I do. I love her."

And that is when it happens.

That is when George presents the situation that enables me to understand—or at least perceive—that I can edit reality.

"Dude, you need to do something," he says, standing up. "You need to be out there. Having some fun. Something to distract yourself."

I remain sitting as he launches into a litany of his own about a charity dance at the WB—a dance he never would have known about had he not answered a survey about his musical tastes and preferences on some social media site—though, of course, the WB no longer exists. The event is meant to celebrate the newly merged communities and to recognize the successful alumni of both schools (now the successful alumni of Consolidated Wallace, the CW) in order to convince said alumni to donate money and time and ego and credence while dancing and participating in an auction . . . emphasis on the "money" part.

"It'll be great," George concludes. "We'll go. We'll laugh at our old teachers. You'll scope the honeys. There were *other* hot girls at the WB, you know."

"I don't want to meet someone else."

"Who said anything about meeting anyone else? You're just window-shopping, is all."

"I don't have any money. I have to find a summer job still."

"We're just going for fun. There will be girls who are going for fun, too. If something happens, it happens. Otherwise, it will be good for a laugh and a great night out, right?"

I have no desire whatsoever to go to the event, nor any desire for "fun" or "great" or anything in that wheelhouse. Yet only moments ago, George held me in his arms while I wept—George, who is no longer a marine, who has seen his life's dream derailed and destroyed for reasons still unexplained and who would still rather talk about my (wreck of a) love life, so I realize—or rather *decide*, as this is now an action I take. George initially attended the WB on scholarship (before his mother's fortunes turned), so perhaps this is why it means so much to him that we attend the event, to offer moral if not financial support.

"Fine," I tell him. "We'll go."

"Dude. Massive. I owe you," he says, and sadly enough, he believes that to be true.

Somehow, I have known that this would/will/must happen.

As George and I step into the auditorium of the WB for the last time (not because we will never return, but because after tonight the building will be renamed and rechristened with CW signs and plaques, a new logo and typeface), I experience déjà vu. Or something like it: a premonitory sense of awareness, simultaneously mindful that I have both experienced this before and have not, yet am about to experience it again . . . for the first time. I remember the dream/vision that I discussed with George while on his porch more than a year ago, remember him reaching for another Stella Artois, remember the night of the dream (the man with the scrambled name, the warning of Inframan, *clean is my anagram*), and that's when I smell it.

Chocolate syrup.

The stench is so strong and so pervasive that I feel as though I've bathed in it—as though everyone around me has bathed in it—and I struggle under the welter of memory and sense and sensation to remember the specifics of the dream/vision so that I can be prepared when George grabs my arm.

"Oh no," George says. "Dude, oh. I didn't know. Don't look."

It is the surest way to guarantee that I will look.

I see Phil, of course. Inevitable, I suppose, as Phil, too, loved/loves her school/alma mater. And of course I see that she is with *him*—*his* arm linked with hers as they enter the auditorium. Phil is wearing a familiar red dress, and even though it looks terrible on her, I still cannot help but to feel a tug toward her, a pull that is as unintentional and irresistible as the gravity that keeps the dumb moon yoked to the earth, the senseless earth yoked to the sun.

"Dude, I should have realized she would be here," says George. "I'm sorry."

"It's all right," I tell him. I'm not lying, either. I am realizing as I say it that it is, in reality, the truth, that it *is* all right that Phil is here, that I am actually *glad* she's here, for now she will be forced to deal with me, to deal with me not as a voiceless, disembodied series of emails or texts, but rather to deal with my physical presence.

Will that change things? Her presence has affected me. Will my presence, in some sort of Newtonian seeking of balance, have an effect on her?[21]

"The red one is all wrong," I tell George. "She should have worn the teal."

He rolls his eyes at me and laughs. "Dude, so now you're a fashion critic?"

Discomfited by the mysterious phantom smell of chocolate syrup—but determined now to ignore it—I steel myself to respond. But before I do, I look back to her, just to prove that I can do so, and my heart hammers at the sight of Phil, no longer in red.

No longer in red at all.

Now clothed in the teal dress I love so much.

21. By "Newtonian," Mike is thinking "equal and opposite," but that would most likely mean that Phil would feel intense hate for Mike, commensurate to the love he feels for her. Probably not the effect he was/is hoping for.

PART II

CHAPTER 10

None of that, of course, was or could be the beginning. Our tales do not begin with Chapter 1 any more than skyscrapers (or underwater hotels) begin on their first stories—there are basements and subbasements, and let us not forget the essential foundation, the digging and reinforcing and buttressing required before even the subbasement can be framed, before even the concrete can be poured. Even the foundation cannot be said to be the beginning, for to begin the foundation, first ground must be broken. To build up, one must first dig down deep. And before *that*? One must plan. There is the site selection; there are blueprints—electrical and plumbing, mechanical—before which comes the architect, the design . . . before which comes the *desire*: the urge to build in the first place. The idea.

All this before the foundation is laid. All before the first story.

DJ Tea, hired for the occasion, spun up a new disc, an old song: "I Want to Hold Your Hand." He plays only 45s, the tiny records a perfect fit for his famously freakishly small hands.

I watched Phil dance to its aged rhythms with *him*, the reek of chocolate syrup slowly abating. The dress was teal; it had always been so. Yet I could recall both realities: red and teal. Two worlds: each equal and valid.

"Dude, are you going to be okay if I leave you alone for a couple minutes?" George asked. "I see some people I want to talk to, but I don't want to leave if you're . . . You know what I mean?"

"I'm fine. Go ahead."

As I stood alone, I could not help but to watch Phil and *him*, and to muse on how my thoughts had begun to clear, to become slightly more coherent in my own skull, perhaps as though the realization that I could edit reality allowed me to edit my thoughts into something more sensible. How far could I go? Was I limited only to changing Phil's wardrobe? No, that was impossible. Because when I changed her dress, *she* changed it, too. Something had happened to *her*, retroactively, to cause her to choose one over the other, and then the other over the one. In other words, I had, in some unknowable way, edited reality such that I changed *Phil* . . . herself, her thought process, her decision-making apparatus. The dress color had not changed as of the moment of my thinking it—the dress changed as of the minutes/hours/days when Phil selected which garment to wear to the WB.

I went dizzy with the implications.

Could I make Phil realize she loved me? Perhaps more important: *Should* I? I knew that she *had* loved me, in a past unmolested by my editing. Was there harm in restoring that *status quo ante*? I could not imagine any reason why not . . . unless in the doing I somehow hurt Phil. But how could this hurt her? Phil had been happy with me, after all. She loved me then, and if all I do is reclaim *then* and insert it into *now*, have I done anything wrong? Is it control or dominance to reassert a prior truth?

I could fix it, so long as I was willing to take the chance.

I watched Phil and *him* on the dance floor until *he* left. *He* kissed her on the lips, a single intimate peck, and then headed toward the bathrooms.

I stopped thinking about reality and my ability to edit it. I ran to her.

"We have to talk," I gasped breathlessly.

She gave me a sour once-over, the way someone might glance at a grocery store bin full of overripe fruit. "We don't have anything to talk about."

My flabby body wilted. "Just for a second, okay? I don't want to be a pain in the ass or anything. I just have to ask you something."

"Mike. Look." She glanced over her shoulder, the universal sign for *PLEASE LEAVE ME ALONE.* "We don't have anything to talk about. Maybe another time. Not tonight. I'm just trying to have fun tonight."

"I understand. And I promise, I'm going to let you get back to your fun. I just have to ask you a very simple question . . ." I realized then that there were, in fact, so many questions I wished to ask Phil. There was no one, single obvious question; there were, instead, a multitude of them. "Phil, please," I finally managed. "Just one question. Something strange is happening. Just tell me why you wore *that* dress. What were you thinking?"

She pulled away from me, eyes narrowed, lips set in a grim line. "Stop it, Mike. You're just embarrassing yourself. I did *not* wear this for you."

"Fine. Fine! Then why? Why did you wear it?"

"Enough!" she hissed. "I'll tell you. And then you leave me the hell alone for the rest of the night. The teal is my favorite, and I look good in it. And if you must know, *he* likes me in it. I'm sorry if that hurts you."

It did, and she knew it. I plowed ahead. "But did something *make* you decide—"

"I just *told* you. Now, seriously—enough. I don't want to be a bitch or anything, but if you keep this up, I'm going to go find a security guy."

"Phil—"

"Leave me alone, Mike."

I turned her dress red. And as I did, Phil proceeded to the bar, still in her red dress, which I'd not changed back. It no longer mattered, though. Not the dress. Not the pain of her last remark to me. Nothing mattered unless I decided it mattered. I would fix everything. I could fix it all. After watching *him* return to the dance floor, I went into the bathroom and did something I hadn't done since telling my weeping self the absolute truth in my College Y bathroom, which felt so long ago as to have been another life. In fact, as I prepared to do it, my heartbeat skipped and jumped as worry thrilled me. Was this like my last name? Like the internal narrator? Was I facing another Third Wall?

I took a deep breath.

I looked in the mirror.

I saw myself. Only myself.

I had been worried that perhaps I would not recognize myself, that in addition to not knowing my own last name, it would turn out that I also did not know what I looked like. But such was not the case—I saw nothing more exotic or exciting or frightening than my own face staring back at me in the mirror.

I thought of the Third Wall and I thought of the internal narrator's voice, and I wondered if these had been forerunners—vanguards, heralds—of my ability to edit reality. Were they preparing me for this day, when I would realize my editorial power over the world? Or had those earlier quirks of nature and reality merely been indicators that I was predisposed to this talent? Were there others like me? If more than one person edited reality, whose edit prevailed? Was what I was going to attempt in any way dangerous? Forcing Phil back to me against her will?

No. I would not impose my will on her and simply change her emotions with the easy facility with which I'd changed her dress. Instead, I would fix what *I* had done and said, the mistakes I had made to lead us to this point. As a result, her love would return naturally, of its own accord.

The smell of chocolate syrup returned, this time overwhelmingly. I tightened my grip on the cool porcelain of the sink. I gagged. I thought again of her dress—currently red. But I remembered the teal. When I edited reality and let it take its course into a new reality and love between Phil and me, I would still remember breaking up with her. I would still remember the months at College Y without her. I would still remember the spring break visit and all its confusion and the heartache that followed and the tears and the hopelessness and the yearning and the denial. I would remember this alongside new memories of Phil, just as I remembered the red dress and the teal dress. Two sets of memories, perpetually. Could I withstand that? The duplicity and the overlap and the cognitive dissonance?

The odor was so thick in my nose and in my sinuses that I felt congested with it, as if I had a chocolate infection commandeering my head. But I had to press on. I spigoted water into my cupped hands and drank it, its metallic tang cutting the chocolate scent that had migrated to my throat and tongue and become a horribly bittersweet taste.

It was time. I looked in the mirror again.

I knew exactly what I had to change . . .

I love you, Phil, or—
   This was a mistake, Phil, or—
   Did you really just come here for a shower? or—
   Are you seeing anyone? or—
   Does this mean we're back together? or even—
   What the hell, Phil?
I stop it there.

I could go on and on. I am sublimely aware of every thought I had at that moment. I am aware of the universes and timelines spinning up and out from my speech, spiraling into their own infinities.

"Phil," I say, breaking the timeline, "I love you."

On doing so, I am inserting the cursor of me into the running text of reality—back to the dorm room, back to spring break, back to when she showed up in my room to take a shower. It is "now" all over again. It is time as redefinition, as a call to action. Across time, it is time to change what happened.

She turns slowly.

Then she freezes in time, in space, in everything.

Am I making the world stand still? Is this what I've done? I choke back the stench of chocolate syrup, so powerfully thick that I want to blurt, "How can you not *smell* that?" but I remain silent instead, silent and just as frozen as she, until she says:

"What did you say?"

"I said I love you."

"Where the . . ." A head shake. A confused working of the lips. "Where did this come from, Mike? You've barely spoken to me in *months*. Where the hell did this come from?"

Needless to say, this is scarcely the reaction I anticipated. I anticipated a rush into my arms. A gasping of "I love you, too!" A barrage of
kisses, an onslaught of desire.

"I don't love you. I'm sorry. I don't love you. I'm with someone else."

The same words. The exact same words she used before, using them
earlier now. The smell of chocolate has faded, leaving behind only the
faint tang of our sex and Phil's soap-clean skin.

"You're with *him*," I say, unable to believe the words even as they
leave my mouth, unable to believe the truth of them, denying the truth
of them.

For the first time since I spoke, she looks not-angry. She looks
shocked.

"Yes," she says at last, wondering how I could know this as desperately as I am wondering why she would come here to fuck me when
she is back with *him*.

"You don't love him," I tell her, remembering my conversation with
George, a conversation that has yet to happen and now may never
happen. "You said you're *with* him, not that you *love* him."

"Who I love doesn't matter," she says after a pause that feels like a
page break in a novel, but isn't. Because it is the same scene, the same
now. "What matters is that I don't love you."

"You came here. You came to see me."

I want to tell her what I've done. I want to explain. But I can't.
Because, after all . . . she came here of her own volition. And that's the
whole point. Before I ever interceded, before I ever interrupted myself,
before I rewrote my actions, she still came *here*. With *him*.

"I don't understand, either," I tell her, pulling away from the tangle
of us.

What must follow will not be pleasant. I know how it will end. I
know I want to avoid that ending. And so I end it here.

CHAPTER 11

Back in the then/now of the WB bathroom, I felt certain that I would barf.

What was going on, anyway? Why the chocolate? Why did it seem as though Willy Wonka (the creepiest and most recent cinematic version thereof) had poured his factory-produced magical brown goo down my throat? Why was I still staring at myself?

I leaned over the sink and told myself to get a grip. I might have even said out loud, "Get a grip, Mike." (Or something similarly idiotic.) The stink of chocolate began to fade. *Thank God.* Head down, I raised my palms in penitence for whatever crime I'd committed to offend this aforementioned God. With tepid water overflowing cupped hands, I wondered if my churning stomach could tolerate a drink of water . . . and as I drew a shaky breath, the door swung open.

"Hey," a voice growled.

There was no need to look up into the mirror. It was *him*. Of course *he* locked the bathroom door behind us, and my thoughts became grounded, as they always had in the past.

I turned off the faucet. "What do you want?"

He came closer to me, an arm's length away. "She told me."

I waited.

"About spring break," *he* added unnecessarily.

Strange: I didn't know what to say here. I felt as if I were missing a line in a teleplay. There had to be a witty rejoinder, a self-deprecating joke, an insult to provoke violence . . . but *he* was already throwing the punch. It landed with tremendous force along the left side of my jaw, rocking me back and to the right, where I collided with the sink and my head bonked against the mirror. *He* advanced.

Why was I still staring at myself?

The stench of chocolate syrup overwhelmed me. He reared back to punch me again and I looked down to see water flowing into the sink. My jaw was no longer sore.

Head down, I raised my palms in penitence for whatever crime I'd committed to offend this aforementioned God. With tepid water overflowing cupped hands, I wondered if my churning stomach could tolerate a drink of water . . . and as I drew a shaky breath, the door swung open.

"Hey," a voice growled.

There was no need to look up into the mirror. It was *him*. Of course *he* locked the bathroom door behind us, and my thoughts became grounded, as they always had in the past.

I turned off the faucet. "What do you want?"

He came closer to me, an arm's length away. "She told me."

I waited.

"About spring break," *he* added unnecessarily.

Strange: I didn't know what to say here. I felt as if I were missing a line in a teleplay. There had to be a witty rejoinder, a self-deprecating joke, an insult to provoke violence . . . but *he* was already throwing the punch, as I knew he would. In the same instant, I brought up my left hand, knocking aside *his* fist. A tingle of pain shot down my arm to my elbow; otherwise I was unhurt. Then came *his* left hook, as I'd also foreseen. So there was no need even to defend the blow. I simply ducked out of the way. *He* nearly fell down, thrown off balance.

We were face-to-face again.

I coughed discreetly; the rancid odor of chocolate syrup clotted my throat. The sludge of time oozed past us while *he* gaped at me—lungs heaving, teeth gritted, fists clenched. "Just watch yourself." (A gasp.) "I won't let you ruin this. You hear me? Phil is mine now. Stay away from her."

I shrugged. The conversation was over. No line was required. Still, as *he* backed away from me, I almost smiled at this modicum of masculine respect I had not expected, nor entirely deserved. Deflecting *his* blow was a consequence not of any skill on my part, but rather on the fact that I'd known it was coming. *He* unlocked the door and left the bathroom, left me wondering if I had edited properly, if I had at last done it *right.*[22]

I tried again, this time seeking to change things such that he never entered the bathroom in the first place, thereby placing myself in a less vulnerable position. But I was incapable of making that change.

A memory came to me just then.

It wafted through my mind and then drifted away, dissipating like the smell of chocolate that now haunted me regularly. A memory from earlier in the evening, when I had wondered, *What if I am not the only one who can edit reality?*

What if, indeed.

More important, What if I was not the only one *actually* editing reality?

I hurried from the bathroom and found George near the bar, chatting with someone I did not recognize. A guy. Intimidating. Beefy but tall, good-looking, blond, about our age.

George introduced him as "Seth, a great linebacker for UPN."

The guy blushed a furious red. Then he seized my hand with such force that I winced. Just as quickly, he let it go, mumbling in a Darth Vader–like baritone, "Nah, man. Those sacks, it was just Seth being in the right place at the right time."

I blinked.

I wasn't imagining things. Seth had just referred to himself in the third person, the same way I (probably) had back in the bathroom in a fit of lunatic idiocy. I was half tempted to say: *Get a grip, Seth.* But Seth was oblivious. So was George. Or something else. Flirtatious? I frowned

22. In *Unedited*, Mike attempts multiple edits during his fisticuffs in the bathroom with *him*, one time memorably resulting in blinding *him*. Eventually, as here, he is able to edit himself into a scenario where no one is hurt.

at him as he punched Seth's shoulder—assuring Seth that Seth was, in fact, a terrific linebacker, definitely the best "who knocked me [George] on my ass! You know what I mean?"

No, I didn't know what he meant.

Seth sneered at me, and then he was gone.

"Dude," George said, "are you all right? Is everything okay?"

Before I could answer, Phil approached. I turned to George; he was gone. But Phil was in red. Definitely in red. I should have been prepared for her appearance—she just walked by me to go to the bar!—and yet for some reason, she caught me off guard. My heart triple-timed, and I felt woozy.

"Mike?" she said.

"Yes?" I managed.

"I just wanted to thank you for not making a scene tonight," she said.

I didn't trust myself to speak. I *had* made a scene. Scenes. Repeatedly. Only no one but me would ever remember because I'd edited them out.

"And I'm sorry about what I said before. About you not acting like a friend lately. I know it's been rough. I would like us to be friends, if you think you can handle that. I just don't want to hurt you. I don't—"

"Phil, it's all right," I heard myself say. "It's going to be all right."

And it would be, I knew. I would fix things. I would find a way to edit the story of Phil and the story of me so that we would be together again.

No. Not "again." I would fix it so that "again" would not be necessary, so that there would be no caesura in our relationship, but rather a smooth continuum. "Again" only applies to something that has ended and then restarted. I would see to it that endings and new beginnings were unnecessary. Because . . .

There is me at College Y, sullen, quiet, standoffish. Soon, friendless, laughless, hopeless.

And, yes, there is me at spring break, alone until Phil mysteriously arrives to fuck me one last time, her actions the same despite the rancor of our parting.

And there is me at the WB event with George, watching Phil and *him*.

And there is me, and me, and only, only forever—

I bolted from the dance and ran to the train.

iCLOUD HACK SUCCESSFUL!

Downloading contents of email exchange between
AUTHOR (Barry Lyga) and EDITOR

FROM: Barry Lyga
TO: *** *********
SUBJECT: Another big problem

Hi, ***!

I hate to be That Guy. I really do. I pride myself on being as chill to work with as possible. But as I'm reading through the little book (I know you hate when I call it that, but to me *Unedited* is the "big book," and so, perforce, this one has to be "the little book") there's a big glaring issue that crops up right in the middle of Chapter 11. (Which is perhaps appropriate, as Chapter 11 is the first chapter in *Unedited*.)

In the second scene in that chapter, Mike recounts, "I tried desperately to imagine a scenario that could return Phil to me. Nothing I had attempted worked."

By this point in *Unedited*, he's edited reality all KINDS of times. And just absolutely messed things up. The world is seriously fucked as a consequence of his edits: in this edited reality, he was NEVER in a relationship with Phil, she thinks he's a stalker, the world's supply of love is running out . . . It's awful.

But in the little book, we just JUMP to that, with no explanation. The story proceeds as though Mike were desperate, as though he's fucked up beyond measure, but we haven't SEEN him make all of those (failed) attempts.

How will readers know/understand everything that has happened, everything he's been through???

LMK your thoughts . . .

Barry

FROM: *** *********
TO: Barry Lyga
SUBJECT: RE: Another big problem

I don't know. We'll think of something, I guess.

Later I sat on the subway, the lone rider in the early morning, deep underground, where the sun could not shine on me even as it rose. I tried desperately to imagine a scenario that could return Phil to me.

Nothing I had attempted worked.

And I had attempted *so much.* Including my most recent, most foolish assay, returning to our intermingled childhoods and confessing my love for Phil upon our first meeting, an act of emotion so large and so improbable that I was certain it would repair the damage I had inadvertently caused.

Instead, I found myself in a world in which Phil—understandably shocked by a stranger's amorous declaration of fidelity and adoration—recoiled from me and henceforth declared me "that crazy guy," going so far even as to swear out a restraining order against me, elongating the already intolerable distance between us.

And so, I am "that crazy guy," a felony-adjacent lunatic with poor impulse control and even poorer judgment. In my desperation, I have worsened the situation, not repaired it.

Was it possible that Phil and I were not meant to be together? That we were destined to be apart, to have our relationship end, whether by her hand or by mine?

Does amorphous, impersonal Destiny supersede individual intention and choice? Can it? Must it?

It was not the first time I'd considered such an idea. Einstein once famously said that God does not play dice with the universe; I could not believe that the universe played dice with me. Even with the weight of so much evidence bearing down on me, I could not shake the idea that Phil and I were meant to be together. Why else would I have been given this power, this perspective on the world, if not to rectify the great wrong done to/by me? More important than destiny was desire: I loved Phil. I wanted/needed to be with her. Desperately. If destiny decreed us apart, then I would defy destiny. Gladly—

The subway clanged and banged to a halt, jostling me from my reverie.

The speaker crackled to life. "Ladies and gentlemen!" a voice blared from above. "This is the final stop on this train. All passengers must disembark. This train is now out of service."

Wait . . . what the hell? How had this happened?

I stood, blinking around at my surroundings: sick-green plastic benches, worn chrome poles to hold, a flecked blue laminate floor. Advertisements at the ends and above the benches, hawking Spanish-as-a-second-language classes, confidential AIDS-II hotlines, adult reeducation classes at the local community colleges. It was all old, all familiar, yet it was as though I were seeing it for the first time.

I disembarked, as instructed. Mild panic set in when I realized I was at the Crimson Rocks subway station: the final stop on the Fox line. I hadn't been here since a field trip in elementary school. I made my way to a flight of stairs that led down, under the desert, then twisted around themselves and rose again to the opposite platform, where trains head back into the city.

No train waited, however. I stood for long minutes, waiting. A poster taped to a nearby column showed a cartoon silhouette of a scorpion, its tail poised to strike. Above the cartoon:

CITY TRANSIT
DEPT. OF TRACKS AND TUNNELS

Below the cartoon, in large, red letters:

CAUTION!

Then:

THIS AREA HAS BEEN BAITED
WITH ARACHNICIDE

Further below that were the details of the date on which the arachnicide had been placed (two days previous) as well as contact information for the DOTAT office responsible for said placing.

With perfect timing, as if to mock both the poster and me, a large scorpion lazily skittered over the track below me.

I heard footsteps. A transit employee was approaching, face stern, his dark polyester uniform vaguely reminding me of a hearse driver. I waved. He stopped.

"I'm just trying to get back to the city," I called to him. "I missed my stop."

"I can't help you with that." He glanced at his watch. "You'll need to get out of here now. This station is closed."

"Closed?"

"This station is closed at this time. Orders from up top."

"Why?"

He shrugged. "I don't ask, kid. I just do what the boss tells me. This early in the morning, no one's going from Crimson Rocks to the city anyway. It'll be about an hour until they open up the line and send a train back into the city."

I considered my options. And then I exited, out into the desert.

To the west loomed the Crimson Rocks, high peaks that offered a primordial mirror image of the city. They were not actually red, of course. They had been named for their discoverer, Lord Crimson, a British expatriate who was the first white man to cross this desert back in the nineteenth century.

I began to walk. I thought of Phil the whole time, sorting out my memories of our various relationships, of the liminal spaces between them, of the ways in which I had tried to fix or change things, always failing. Remembered her as Othello[23], as Estragon. Remembered her confident and nigh imperious on the set, commanding, ordering, coaching her fellow actors into a diorama she held entirely in her mind, the way I held blueprints. We were so much the same, she and I. Both builders. Both artists. And she had all the confidence I lacked.

---

23. Phil's gender- and race-bent portrayal of the Moor is still spoken of in hushed tones wherever dramatic artists convene.

I thought of the time she'd texted me: *come snuggle w/me & listen 2 the rain.*

Rain is rare in the desert.

That night, she wanted me to come lie in bed with her and listen to the rain on her roof.

As much as I tried right now—right *then*, whenever, in this moment, with the rising sun at my back—I could not remember why I had denied her. Or denied *myself.* I pined for the chance to hold her in my arms and let the rain lullaby us to sleep. And yet that small, simple thing was beyond me for reasons I could no longer recall . . .

Was that the moment? Was that the crucial moment in our relationship? Did I need to edit that moment and go to her, arrive gently wet with desert rain at her front door, kiss her, slip into the history-made sheets with her and just . . . hold her? Was that the secret?

I did not know.

I could not know.

I had tried so many times, seeking to reunite us, to conjoin us, and had ended only alone and alone and alone.

I sat down in the sand, staring ahead at the Crimson Rocks, staring through them at what lay beyond. Out there in the desolation of the desert, in the shadow of my own city, trapped between its familiar skyscrapers and the Crimson Rocks, all things seemed possible and impossible at once, I felt as though I could become George's best friend there. I felt as though I could—finally—recapture lost Philomel there.

No, not Philomel. Never Philomel. Only Phil.

I needed help.

I had tried this on my own and had nothing to show for it but endlessly entangled strands of fate, reality, life, love, history. A Gordian knot I refused to cut through. I would live this. I would succeed. But . . . right now/then, I needed help. So I swiped open my cell phone and called George, who answered on the first ring.

"Dude," he said.

"George, I'm sorry to bother you," I jabbered breathlessly, "but I need your help, man. I really, really need your help."

"Are you in jail? Is that it? Do you need me to bail you out? You know what I—"

"No. I'm at Crimson Rocks."

"What?" His voice perked up. "Why . . . How do you have a cell signal way out there?"

"I don't know. But we need to talk, okay? Please, George. I'm sorry to wake you up, but—"

"You didn't. I'm still . . . Look, come on over, dude. Mom'll make us something to eat."

"No. You need to come *here*."

"What?"

"Please, George. Please come here. Now."

I killed the call before he could respond. As I shoved my phone back in my pocket, I lifted my head and looked around at the endless desert . . . at the cacti and the rocks and dunes and arroyos. I thought of wandering, of the endless possibility of the sky above—turning now from sapphire to the pink-blue that comes right after the dawn—the clouds clustered among the peaks of the Crimson Rocks, like eager patrons waiting for the show to start . . . so tired of the opening act, waiting for something to begin.

And something *would* begin. Soon.

Something was coming.

A surprise was coming.

I knew that, because I remembered it. And that was when I realized something else. I'd recently forgotten my own last name. Or perhaps I'd never known it. And right now, I couldn't remember the name of the city in which I lived. In which Phil lived. In which Mike lived. In which my family—

My family. My family?

I don't know my parents' names. I don't know my brother's name. I don't know who they are.

And the city itself . . .

I spun in a circle, turning the desert on the axis of me. Where *was* I? Where was *this*? Who was I, and why was the world suddenly making no sense?

And why did it make sense that the world made no sense?

"Dude!"

I whirled to see George emerging from the subway station. I wasn't sure how much time had passed. The sun was higher in the eastern sky now; George's shadow seemed to shrink as he approached.

"Okay," he grumbled. "I'm here. What the hell is going on?"

For a moment, I said nothing. George—his brief rant expelled—calmed; he shaded his eyes with his hand and gazed out at the Crimson Rocks.

"Shit. Haven't been here since . . ." He trailed off, whether because he could not remember or did not care to remember, I could not tell. "Why'd you drag me out here, man?"

He stood ramrod straight, one stiff hand held at his brow. I could not help but to imagine him in his marine uniform and to wonder, however briefly, at what had caused him to leave the corps so soon after entering.

When he caught me staring, he sank next to me in the sand.

"Go," he said after a moment.

I gave myself a few seconds.

"Think about where we live."

He twisted around and cast his gaze back toward the city, which reared behind us, backlit by rising sunshine. "What about it?"

"Well . . . where do we live, George?"

He stared at me. "What are you talking about? We live in the city." He pointed to it, as though I'd forgotten where it was.

"But *what* city? What's it called?"

He waved it off. "Dude, you're being an idiot. Like you were with your application. Why does this stuff matter to you? It never mattered before."

"Right! My application! But before *what*? When?"

He scowled at me. "When we were kids," he said.

"George, we never *were* kids! It's all flashbacks, man. It's all stuff we *think* happened, but there's no context for any of it. Nothing happened *around* it. They're just discrete memories."

"And this has what to do with the city?"

Frustrated, I grabbed him by the shoulders and oriented him to see what I saw. "The city's skyscrapers all scream *East Coast of the United States*. But the residential buildings—the houses we live in—are all bungalow-style and fake adobe and fake hacienda. They scream *West Coast*. No one designs cities like that, George. It's insane. It doesn't happen by accident, and it sure as hell doesn't happen by design. So I want to know where the fuck we live. Where is there a city with skyscrapers *and* bungalows . . . in a desert . . . with a subway? Where *is* this place?"

He smirked, and I knew he was going to make a crack about architecture.

"It's not about architecture," I said.

Instead of responding, he sighed again. Then he turned away and ran some sand through his fingers, staring out at the Crimson Rocks.

"Look at me," I said.

He shook his head.

"*Look at me*," I repeated, the way his former marine sergeant might have barked an order.

George turned. And before I could change my mind, I began to confess.

"I don't know how to explain it. Somehow, I have this . . . *power*. For lack of a better word. This ability. I can change things. It's like I go back and find specific moments and just tweak reality a little bit, and then everything proceeds differently. But I went too far and I fucked it all up. Now nothing makes sense. I can't keep track of it anymore."

It was as though I'd just thrown up, by which I mean I felt terrific. I'd purged the sickness. Or I'd made a start. And even though I thought I'd said everything I could/would/needed to say, it turned out I had more in me, for the next thing I knew, I was telling George the entire story— all of it—from the beginning at the WB with the red-now-teal-now-red dress to the smell of chocolate to the dream to the repeated revising of reality that had brought me to this place, to summon George and try to fix the mess I'd made of my world.

"I'm not crazy," I finished, nearly gasping. "Everything I'm telling you is true."

Something shifted in his eyes, though nothing I'd said was entirely persuasive. "I guess I owe you the benefit of the doubt," he said, "after everything you've done for me. You know what I mean? Even though you've never read any Gayl Rybar."

I winced with guilt, the pain of it nearly physical. I had done nothing for George, and the Gayl Rybar reference was deliberate, a pointed barb, its subtext clear: *You haven't even done* that, *Mike.* He owed me nothing; I owed him everything. And yet here I was again, imploring him to believe me, to help me.

"So let's just say I'll suspend disbelief.[24] How does it work?" he asked. "It's like you go back in time and change things?"

"No. Not like that. I don't know how to describe it. It's more like editing things. Like I can see the structure of reality and manipulate it."

He rolled his eyes. "How is that different from time travel?"

"It just is. I don't have total control over it. It's like there are only certain points I can alter, as if it's already been decided and I'm just going through the motions. I have this control, but I don't really control anything. I feel like someone else is editing, too, maybe at the same time, guiding me to try different things."

He folded his arms over his chest and considered. "Well . . . okay. Look, dude. Let's assume you're not nuts, all right?"

"I appreciate that."

"Let's say you can do this stuff. Show me. Prove it."

"I can't."

He raised an eyebrow, a disbelief-not-suspended eyebrow.

"George, seriously! Look, it's not that I can't—it's just that it doesn't

---

24. "Suspension of disbelief" is a term bandied about by authors and editors—and, more important, the many millions of readers of fiction who care about such things—to describe the process by which a reader of fiction accepts an implausible universe into which they are dropped. How's that working out for you right about now?

matter if I do. To you, I've always been obsessed with Phil. I made a change to Phil and you didn't notice because you're within it all. It's like . . . I'm erasing something and putting in something new. *You* don't notice what's missing, only what's there."

He nodded, mute.

Did you think it would be that easy?

He wasn't asking the question. It was the voice from my dreams.

"It was the kid," I said.

George blinked at me. "What kid? What are you talking about?"

"The kid. With the ice cream cone. I saw him on the subway. *After* I dreamed about him. After, George! It was in the dream. That's when I walked down the hallway made of ice. And that's when the kid talked to me. Inframan. He said he was called Inframan. Der Untermensch. The Underone. The God of Failure. Inframan. That's what he said, George. That's what . . ."

I was done.

George stood and smiled at me, reaching out a hand. "Let's get you home," he said.

"I messed it all up, George," I rasped, my voice spent. "I love Phil."

CHAPTER 12

I did not remember coming home or crawling into bed to sleep, but I supposed I owed George for this, too. My face felt grimy and dry with old tears as I became conscious of my cell phone ringing.

"Dude," George said when I answered. "Are you at your computer?"

"Give me a sec," I said.

"Type in that stuff you told me before," George instructed as I groggily logged on. "Search it. Inframan. Untermensch. The Underone. See what comes up."

There were only a few hits. They all seemed related. The first one was:

INFRAMAN (subtitle: "The Coming of the Unpotent God") is the first book by American novelist Barry Lyga, published in 1994. www.wikinformation.com/inframan-novel

"Have you ever heard of this guy Barry Lyga?" George asked.

"No. Never."

"Are you sure? Because when you put in all of those words, all that comes up is stuff related to him and this book of his. Scroll to the bottom."

I'd stopped listening. Because I was seized with . . . something. Not dread. Not déjà vu. Not excitement. A freakish combination thereof. The images on the screen were the images of the dead man I'd seen in the dream with the ice cream boy.

"Mike?" George asked in the silence.

"This is the guy!" I cried. "The guy who was dead and then alive and then dead again."

"So you have heard of him, then."

"No, that's just it! I've never heard of him before. But . . ." I stared at the picture. It was definitely the man from my dream. He looked somehow older and heavier in the photo, but it was still unquestionably the same person.

George offered me a grim chuckle. "Dude, check out the page. Barry Lyga's dead."

****

Barry Lyga

From Wikinformation, the world's finest info dump!

Barry Lyga (no middle initial) (September 11, 1971–August 5, 2005) was an American novelist and short-story writer. Lyga majored in English at Yale receiving his BA in 1993. His first novel, *Inframan*, was written when he was a senior and published in 1994. The book is notable mainly for influencing the work of nonadult author Gayl Rybar.

Contents

1 Personal Information

2 Death

3 Works

   3.1 *Inframan*

   3.2 *The Sunday Letters and Other Stories*

I put my phone on speaker and set it on the desk so that I could press both palms to my temples, as though holding in my brains, finally understanding the expression "mind-blowing."

"Dude, you still there? Did you hear me? The guy's dead. Died back in—"

"Yeah. I see it—2005." I did some quick mental math. "He was thirty-three."

"Look," George said, "I don't know what any of this means. I think you need to get some more sleep, and you need to move on, you know what I mean? You need to forget about Phil. You need to find someone else, okay?"

I barely heard him. My eyes skipped along the page, my fingers scrolling the trackpad. Dead. He was dead. Had been dead for years. How had I known? I had dreamed him dead. But I had also dreamed him alive. And then dead again. And then . . .

"Mystery solved," George said. His voice didn't sound friendly. His voice sounded like judgment. "You heard about this guy from someone, and you dreamed about him. End of story. If you'd actually read some Gayl Rybar, like I've been begging you to for years, none of this would have been an issue at all."

I clicked on the link for his first book, *Inframan.*

To proceed, I had to enter my email address and allow LonelyDude to send me some more information.

"George," I said, my voice so quiet that I had to say it again before he acknowledged. "George, is my last name Grayson?"

"Yeah. Mike Grayson. Why?"

****

Inframan (novel)

From Wikinformation, the world's finest info dump!

Inframan, or The Coming of the Unpotent God is the first book by American novelist Barry Lyga, published in 1994. The novel is a metafiction about a character named Mike Grayson and his friends and family.

Contents

1 Plot

2 Characters

****

In my dream, Barry Lyga was dead. Then alive. I met a child who called himself Inframan.

And now . . .

Now I find that the main character in Lyga's first novel has the same name as I do.

I wanted to slam shut the laptop and crawl back into bed. I wanted to forget I'd ever dreamed of Lyga or of Inframan.

"George. Did you see . . . the name of the main character in *Inframan?*"

I waited a moment as he clicked, heard the short, sharp inhale on his end of the line.

"Have you been listening to me?" he nearly shouted. "If you think that's crazy, wait until you see what else I found. Part of the book. Online. I mean, I looked in all the usual ebookstores, but no one had it, but then I found this old blog in a Google cache. Someone who goes by the name of 'gaylwriter'—guess who *that* is—posted a chunk of the novel. It's short, but . . ."

"But what?"

"Well, I think it's gonna blow your mind."

****

gaylwriter says: This next scene is actually one of my least favorite from the entire book, but it's so central to the narrative that I figure it's worth posting. Ham's dream, in which he encounters two versions of Mike Grayson, is almost deliberately scattered and feels somewhat pointless, though it resonates later, especially toward the end of the book. Here it is:

He's walking down a corridor with walls, floor, and ceiling of ice. Strangely, he is not cold, though he is wearing only shorts and tank top. He sees his breath pluming from him in white puffs. In the background, someone is playing what sounds like an electric cello. A woman sings, "Hey, can you peel shrimp? Oh yeah, baby, gotta peel the shrimp."

No problem.

He comes to a door, made of wood, set flawlessly into the surrounding ice, as if it grew there naturally. There are no hinges. When he grasps the doorknob, a voice says, "Not on the first date!"

"I thought there were no quotation marks in dreams," he says.

"Well, of course there are. Think of the consequences," says the voice. See how confusing this is? it says, it says.

"Oh," Ham responds, then reaches for the doorknob again. "NO!" the voice shouts.

"Why not?" he whines.

"Are you wearing a condom?"

Ham pulls out his wallet. "All I have is a diaphragm."

"That'll have to do. Put it in your mouth."

He does so.

"Okay."

Now there is no protest when he turns the knob. The door vanishes, showing the corridor beyond. This hallway is made of wood, built at a skewed angle, such that his left foot is below his right foot, forcing him to walk at an angle. From nowhere, a man's voice sounds out: "I warned them! I told them!"

He finds himself in a large chamber, paneled in oak, carpeted lushly. A fire roars in the fireplace, and several plaques and trophies rest on the mantelpiece. Lying next to the fireplace is a body clad in a gray trench coat and slacks, a heavy black poker protruding from its chest. Ham approaches the corpse. It is Mike.

"Oh man, Mike, oh God, I wish I coulda saved ya—"

"Hey, Ham," the corpse says, opening its eyes, sitting up. "How are you?"

"But—you're dead."

"Not always." His eyes close then, and he falls back, dead.

Ham turns just in time to see a door open. Mike steps into the room, wearing jeans and a brown leather jacket. His hair is slicked back from his forehead. He is holding a wireless microphone in one hand. A spotlight pins him.

"Mike!" Ham cries.

"Mike?" Grayson seems puzzled. He nods, and then gestures with his right hand. "Right here," he agrees, holding the microphone aloft.

"Huh?"

"Look, Hamburg—you don't mind if I call you Hamburg, do you?—I'm going to give you a glimpse, okay?"

"What?"

"A small glimpse, to be sure, but a glimpse nonetheless. Remember something for me, Hamburg. He's just a figment of his own imagination. Can you remember that?"

"I think so."

"Well, don't bother. Hey! Hey, swallow that diaphragm, man. How do you expect to breathe without one?"

"Oh yeah. Right." He swallows it with one gulp.

"Now, rooms don't always have one exit, Hamburg. And houses have many rooms."

"What are you trying to say—"

"It doesn't matter, I guess. Unless you get things going soon, Inframan will kill all of you."

"Who?"

"Inframan."

"Never heard of him."

"Of course not! You think I'm here to tell you things you know? Angia grew up near here." Ham hears a tiny click and then a large, *crystal chandelier plummets from the ceiling, crushing Mike to the floor.*

"Hey, Ham!"

Turning again, Ham sees the impaled Grayson, once again struggling into a sitting position. "Don't listen to him, Ham. Heck, the Dragon's coming."

"Dragon?"

"No, the Dragon. Pay attention. The dead can walk, okay? Can you remember that?"

"Maybe."

"Well, make sure you do. It's important. Birds fly and die."

"They do?"

"I guess; how am I supposed to know? You think I'm making this stuff up? Look, I'll tell you your future, okay? I see gold eclipsing chocolate. Carter's hair stands on end. Isn't this all so very Twin Peaks?"

"I DON'T UNDERSTAND!" Ham screams.

"Don't have a hissy fit, Ham," Mike admonishes him. "After all, it's only life."

The ice corridor . . . the dead-then-alive-then-dead body . . . It was *my* dream, the dream I described to George, only twisted and changed. I felt an overpowering wave of déjà vu and then realized that it was not and could not be déjà vu. This was not the sense that "this has all happened before." It was, rather, the knowledge, the certainty that this had all happened before, only in some different way.

"Is there more?" I asked George. "She says that this is the 'next' scene she's posting. So she must have posted others, right?"

"Her blog isn't up anymore," George said. "But you know who that is, right?"

My mouth was so dry I could only croak the name. "Gayl Rybar?"

George laughed. "It's not even really a blog. It looks like it was some old-school page from, like, 1999 or something. A school project, maybe. I just got lucky and found the cache of that page. Tell you what—I'll keep poking around, see what I can find, and you do the same. I'll call you back in . . . let's say an hour."

Inframan (novel)

From Wikinformation, the world's finest info dump!

Inframan, or The Coming of the Unpotent God is the first book by American novelist <u>Barry Lyga</u>, published in 1994. The novel is a <u>metafiction</u> about a character named Mike Grayson and his friends and family.

Contents

Plot

NOTE: This section contains spoilers.

The plot revolves around the exploits of a New Haven police detective named Mike Grayson and his attempts to find a serial killer named the Shadow Boxer who is hunting students at Yale University. At the same time, however, Grayson begins to notice strange logical incongruities and discontinuities in his life and world, which lead him to the discovery that he is, in fact, merely a character in a novel written by Barry Lyga. As the novel progresses, the search for the Shadow Boxer becomes less and less important, and Grayson and his friends and family find themselves caught between Lyga and Inframan, described as "the Undergod" and "the God of Failure." Inframan turns out to be another version of Lyga (or, perhaps, a split personality) who exercises strict editorial restraint to counterbalance Lyga's creative whims.

The tension between the two forces wreaks havoc with the lives of the characters. In the end, Grayson's love for his sister is powerful enough to reunite the cast, just in time for the Shadow Boxer to fatally shoot Grayson. Grayson then ascends to Heaven, where he learns that Heaven is merely one step below the Real World. He ascends to the Real World and finds himself on the campus of the real Yale University, where he seeks out Lyga in the author's dorm. Lyga, however, is missing from his room, leaving behind only the unfinished manuscript to *Inframan* and a single blank piece of paper, with instructions for Grayson himself to finish the novel.

The novel's conclusion is paradoxically inconclusive, as Grayson (revived from the dead thanks to timely electric shocks delivered by the Electrostatic Man) visits his brother's grave and apparently will live a long, happy life. The final page of the book, though, is clearly written by Lyga, not by Grayson, causing the reader to wonder if the author has deceived and swindled his own character, and if the seemingly happy ending can be trusted.

I returned to the Wikinformation page on Barry Lyga, skimmed it, clicked on the link for *Death*.

Death

On the morning of August 6, 2005, police were called to Lyga's home in Reisterstown, Maryland (a suburb of Baltimore). Lyga

was found dead in the bedroom, having died on the previous
day, August 5. The coroner ruled his death a suicide, but Lyga's
family protested the ruling, pointing out that he was hard at
work on a new novel.

Shortly after releasing the autopsy report, the Baltimore
County Coroner's Office rescinded it, offering no explanation.
Lyga's death therefore remains a mystery, with no cause
of death publicly available. The Baltimore County Police
Department lists the case as "officially open," but "cold."

"He's just gone," I whispered to myself.

I had made myself a cup of tea to drink as I read the site. I squeezed
some lemon into it now, watching the slightly cloudy beads of juice
squirt and drip. I wondered, *Who was Barry Lyga?*

Why did he matter?

PART III

CHAPTER 13

After years of insistence both explicit and veiled, I capitulate to George's wishes: in the absence of books by Barry Lyga (which seem not to exist on any e-reader platform), I read Gayl Rybar.

Books are hideously inefficient conveyors of information. Dense, yes, but difficult to customize without causing damage. They require a rigid left-to-right, page-to-page schema, and random access usually results in bafflement, not enlightenment. Still, I read.

And I begin to understand George's obsession with Gayl Rybar. The books—which, truthfully, I skim rather than outright read, but it's enough to get the gist—are uniformly about outsiders, outcasts, loners. People without a clan or a community, who are forced to build one by accretion and force of will, if not need. I imagine fatherless George, bruises and broken bones healed but never forgotten, peering into these pages, seeing himself reflected in them as surely as in a mirror, seeing that while he may be by himself, he will never be alone.

The books are, quite simply, George's best friend.

With a heavy sigh, I put aside the works of Gayl Rybar, which are useless to me save for their insight into George. Resting near them is my sketchbook, which has been a constant in every version of every edit I've made. Phil has been excised from my life, but architecture remains.

My architecture professor was right, regardless of the world in which he lives. I see that now. I should have taken heed when, at the end of the semester, he wrote TAKE YOUR TIME in neat block letters in my sketchbook.

Staring at those words now, taking a little break from questions of epistemology[25] (as it relates to my own existence), I think, *Easy for you to say.*

I flip back through the pages, examining the design for my underwater hotel, the design that I will forever associate with Phil. Granted, in its sheer complexity, the physics of the hotel trump the economics of it, and in pushing past the practical difficulties, the economics trump the physics. "Anything is possible," my architecture professor was fond of saying. *Oh yeah, you fucking hypocrite?* He should have added, "if you have tenure and can say anything you want," or, "with the liberal and consistent application of money."

Disgusted with him—though mostly with myself—I throw the pad across the room.

This is my fate. Failure is my fate. I will never finish the underwater hotel, because it can never be finished. Even if I manage to reassemble some shambling, cobbled-together Frankenstein's monster of a design, this should not surprise me. Failure is my natural state. I have failed in architecture just as I failed with Phil. Given all the power in the universe, I still could not win her back. Like architecture and physics and money, there may be a way to leverage power to convince someone of love . . . but no. It can't be that I am incompetent and impotent to find it. It's just that love is in short supply, like professors of architecture.

"You win, Inframan," I hear myself whisper.

The God of Failure has succeeded at last. He's defeated me.

And in my defeat, I must figure out how to move on, must find a new path for myself. George is right. I need to forget about her. I need

---

25. Epistemology is the theory of knowledge, the inquiry into its possibility, nature, and structure.

to forge ahead. I want to forget. I wish I could forget. But I have remembered too hard, with too-powerful intent. I cannot forget. I will not forget. In a world of blonds and redheads and brunettes, there is only one sapphire-tressed Phil. Poets and singers and authors call blue the color of depression and despair. For me, blue is the color of love. Of hope.

Blue is Phil, and Phil is blue.

I cannot forsake her. I cannot give up.

I retrieve my drawing pad. Physics is not to economics as Phil is to my story. My designs, my dreams, are solid and true and valid. So, too, is my design for Phil. I flip open the pad and begin to write. I write everything I remember about Phil—not just her physical appearance, but her way of speaking, the way she stood, the things she said to me, the ways she believed, the ways she did not believe. The faith she had in me, the way she wanted to change. How she knew the very best gummi bears. Her shelf of "classic" children's books. Why did I not read them to her when she asked? I would read them all to her now.

Is this not the very definition of love, this recollection of every detail, this knowledge, so complete and so all-consuming? If not, it should be.

Or is this mere obsession, love's drooling, slack-jawed cousin? Is this the path to destruction that Angia Eiphon's dreamer found himself walking?

Obsession cannot stand in for love. Is there anything else that *could*? I put the pad down, suddenly overwhelmed with a sensation I cannot describe, some familiar creature that has evolved to the point that what traditionally had been a nagging sensation at the back of the brain became a subtle bass line in a song that has been amplified to overwhelm the melody, the lyrics, indeed all the other components of the song.

It feels familiar. Something is going to happen. Something is coming—

My phone rings.

The buzzing snaps me back to what I think is reality. It's George, of course. Who else?

"Dude," George says, "are you at your computer?"

"Yeah," I say. "What—"

"Go down the Gayl Rybar rabbit hole," he interrupts. "Because I know you haven't."

Gayl Rybar

Gayl Rybar (no middle initial) (September 11, 1979–) is an American nonadult novelist and short-story writer who is best known as the author of *The Unlikely Tale of Geekster and the Vampiress,* published in 2006.

Contents

1 Personal Information

2 Blog

Personal Information

Gayl Rybar is an American author. According to an interview in *Publishers Daily,* Rybar is currently at work on a novel titled *Unfinished.*

Blog

I want to talk about the very end of the book today. Not the epilogue, but the <u>real</u> end of the book. When Mike ascends to the Real World and goes to Lyga's room at Yale, he finds only a single sheet of paper and a note that reads, "Finish the book yourself." He sits down and we get enough clues that we realize that what he writes ends up being the book's epilogue. It's sort of a clever gambit on Mike's part because it allows him—within the confines of a single page—to not only give himself a happy ending, but also to guarantee one for the rest of the cast.

What follows after that last page, though, is clearly not written by Mike. In a novel that has been built in part on the usage of excerpts from various texts, the true final page of the book stands out for being the only excerpt whose source material is never identified:

The following is an excerpt:

In the end, then, metafiction is the coward's solution for authors. Any flaw in the story, any incomprehensibility, can simply be waved away with the comment that it is intentional, that the reader must forgive these gaffes as they are meant to be part and parcel of the entire story. Such a story, then, is purportedly bulletproof.

Why would anyone want to read such a story?

"Dude," George says, "I keep thinking about 'Clean is my anagram,' you know what I mean?"

I shake my head. I am in my underwear, on my phone, looking at my computer screen. "Did I tell you about that?" I whisper.

Not that it matters. The answer is what matters, and this one is obvious: Another author. But this one is alive. This one is alive and has a name that—when scrambled (or is it unscrambled?)—is the same as Barry Lyga, who is dead. This is completely insane. Gayl Rybar. Another author coming to me from nowhere. Letters. Letters combining and recombining. Mixing. Taking new forms.

I've come this far; I'll go further. I'll find Gayl Rybar and I'll ask her what she knows about Barry Lyga. I'll learn what I can from her, and then I'll take the next step, whatever that is. And then the next step after that. And after that. Whether those steps add up to a mile or a million of them, I will take them all.

"Do you understand why I've always talked about Gayl Rybar? Why I read her?"

"Yes. Yes, I do."

"Good. So then maybe for once you can listen to *me*, okay? Meet me tomorrow at Books-A-Go-Go."

iCLOUD HACK SUCCESSFUL!

Downloading contents of iMessage chat between
AUTHOR (Barry Lyga) and EDITOR

LYGA: So . . . we're just gonna skip the stuff where they go to Maryland and visit the grave of Barry Lyga? All that pseudo-detective work they do to figure out the connection between Barry Lyga and Gayl Rybar?

EDITOR: All of that will still be in *Unedited*. We have to lose some stuff for this book, because this is the story of Mike and Phil. You know that. You knew there would be cuts.

LYGA: I guess I didn't realize how much we would lose in the process.

EDITOR: Sorry, I have to take this call. We'll talk later.

LYGA: I thought you turned your phone off when you were editing.

CHAPTER 14

And as though no time at all has passed, it's the next day, and I meet George at Books-A-Go-Go.

Barry Lyga has no books here. But we do find Gayl Rybar—not one, but two: dual (duel?) paperbacks of *The Unlikely Tale of Geekster and the Vampiress*. The cover is jet-black, with an embossed sheet-white female silhouette that exudes aggression and anger. The title is picked out in varnished letters, black against black, such that the words are legible only by holding the cover at certain angles to the light.

Flipping *The Unlikely Tale* to its first page, I read:

Of all the things I want in the world, there is one that I will never reveal.

I flip to the back. On the inner back cover, there is a short biography of Gayl Rybar, but no author photograph:

The Unlikely Tale of Geekster and the Vampiress is Gayl Rybar's first novel, and it pretty much proves that you can grow up reading picto-novels and still manage to accomplish something with your life. Gayl lives in the city in the desert.

"George," I whisper. "George, look." I grab him by the sleeve and pull him closer, which is hardly necessary as he was standing very close to begin with, yet I pull him still closer and shove the book up to him where he can do nothing but read the inner flap. "See what it says? It says she lives here! Why didn't you ever tell me that?"

"You never listened when I talked about Gayl Rybar," he says, his admonishing words unmatched to his elated tone. He one-arm-hugs me, crushing us together with an almost-intimate strength. "She lives here! We can find her!"

"Are we sure she's a she?"

He gives me a look I've never seen before, a look of disgust. "What do you mean?"

"I'm saying . . . what if Gayl Rybar and Barry Lyga are the same person? She's writing a book titled *Unfinished*. And Barry Lyga died before finishing his last book."

George smiles and nods. "You think he faked his own death, took on a new name, and started a new writing career? You know how batshit crazy that sounds?"

I smile and nod back.

He shrugs. "Only one way to find out. We get to her." George is a whiz at such things, and fortunately, Gayl Rybar has used her address as a privacy unlock, so it was released to the public in a very mundane data-hack and is available on a number of sites. It turns out Gayl Rybar lives only three blocks from a subway stop on the Crimson Rocks line. George bolts outside.

I try to follow him, but my legs turn to sludge outside the bookstore. I can't move.

Impatient, George does an about-face and stomps back down the sidewalk.

"Why are you dragging?" he asks. "This is our chance. Trust me." His eyes narrow. "You *do* trust me, right? We're best friends, Mike. We're brothers."

I am not his best friend, as I have acknowledged. Yet when he claims me as such, I feel for the first time as though I could reciprocate someday—that our relationship *does* transcend such simplistic notions as genetic origin and class (or even more complicated ones . . . like my own self-absorption, like his family dynamic)—and that an opportunity will arise when I can perform some service or action, something to make me worthy of George's best-friend-dom. I sense that it's possible. Or is it?

"Sorry," I say. "My brain just isn't always online these days."

He shrugs. "We can't do anything about it. We can't fix everything."

"Can't we? Can't I? I can edit reality," I say. "Maybe I can learn how to do it right." An idea occurs to me, one that quickens my pulse. "And if *I* can edit it, then I bet other people must be able to! Maybe I can team up with someone else and actually fix things!"

"Hmm?" George has been checking messages on his phone and did not hear me.

"Nothing. Never mind. Let's go find Gayl Rybar." I take a deep breath. Just in saying the words, just in this moment of purpose, I sense a gathering about me, as though the mere act of deciding has placed me—me and George, too; the world, maybe—on a new, inescapable path, a path with no more distractions or divergences. "I have a feeling everything is about to change."

"What do you mean?"

"I'm not sure."

"Then let's wait. Until tomorrow, okay?"

I nod, feeling an indescribable sense of relief—like nothing I've felt before, except for when Phil made the first move, back at that party (it was a party, wasn't it?) . . . all that endless and instantaneous time ago.

"Okay."

PART IV

CHAPTER 15

George stood outside his house.[26] There were piles of wood—two-by-fours, sheets of plywood—stacked in the driveway, as always, like pyramids built to testify to George's mother's ongoing interior redesign project, the piles changing in size and shape and kind of wood (pine, then cherry, then oak, then hickory), but their existence a constant. Ever since the asshole had left—had been made to leave, was more accurate—George's mom had turned the house into a perpetual redesign machine, flowing from the original contemporary design to Victorian to classic to neoclassic to neocontemporary to modern to Georgian to whatever the hell it was now.

Only George's bedroom had gone untouched, every other room in the house twisting and turning and reconfiguring under his mother's insistent and watchful and demanding eye. The hundreds of thousands of dollars she had spent over the years had not touched the outside of the house, only the inside. Even though George had lived almost his entire life in this house, he felt as though he'd hardly lived here at all.

That, he knew, was the point.

We should just sell the house, George had told her during his youth—dodging contractors, trying to study while hammering and drilling and

---

26. Oh, my—we've switched from first-person to third-person. That's weird, isn't it?

sawing whirled around him, safe in his cocoon of a room with the novels of Gayl Rybar—safe from the madness. *We just should sell it and move . . . if you hate it so much.*

Hate it? she'd responded. *I love this house. It's our home. It just needs a little work, is all.*

George understood; he tried to understand. But rejiggering the innards of the house would not change what had happened, nor would it exorcise the ghosts of 911 calls and kicks and punches and slaps; only leaving would accomplish that, but leaving was precisely what his mother refused to do. And he loved his mother—she had asked no questions when he returned from basic training and she had, other than the ceaseless remodeling, never interfered in his life to any appreciable degree, almost as though she were apologizing for the rigid hold that terror had had over his early years by overcompensating via laxity in his later teen years . . . He could not tell her the truth, that he was traipsing off with Mike to look for . . . who knew what? Nor could he tell her nothing and simply disappear . . . nor could he lie.

I'm going somewhere with Mike, he could say.

But she would not accept that. She would say, *Always going somewhere with Mike.*

He's my best friend, Mom, George would offer.

He could tell his mother, he supposed, some variant of the truth: that his regular beatings as a child and the continual witnessing of his mother's torture at the asshole's hands had inculcated in him a desire not to be harmed or defenseless, but at the same time had also imprinted on him an extreme and almost bloodthirsty desire—no, *need*—to protect others; that the pain and shame he'd felt as a child after one of the asshole's beatings was nothing as compared to the shame, weakness, and helplessness he'd felt at being unable to protect his mother from that never-ending torrent of abuse and danger and suffering. People needed protection—George knew that from an early age—and while there had been no one to protect him, he could at least be there to protect others.

And now that the marines were done with him, he would do what he could on his own. Maybe he was nothing more than Mike's sidekick—that was all right. Being a sidekick was actually a noble and time-honored tradition. Don Quixote needed Sancho Panza. Hamlet needed Horatio. Without the sidekicks, without the foils, the Mikes of the world would not and could not shine so bright, nor would they even survive to tell their tales. He would simply tell his mother that he was going to spend some time with Mike, and that was that.

His cell chirped for attention as he entered the house, a text from Seth, the former UPN linebacker he'd seen at the CW celebratory ball the other night.

George stared at the text for a long time. He felt as though two worlds were coming together, worlds that could either collide and destroy each other in a great fury or somehow mesh together and unite, becoming a new, single world in the process. He couldn't imagine the latter happening, and did not want to picture the former, so after a long moment staring at the screen, he dismissed the text message and slid the phone back into his pocket.

"Characters in books exist to suffer," his mom told him later that night.[27] "That's their purpose. They go through things so that we can feel along with them."[28]

George nodded. He felt things he'd never felt before via the writings of Gayl Rybar.

"They go through horrible things so that when they ultimately triumph," she added, "the reader gets to feel a . . . a . . . cathartic buzz, a vicarious victory. Oh, that was alliteration. I know. I want to leave it."

Ultimately triumph . . .

"So they have to win in the end?" George asked. That sounded promising for Mike. For everyone, really.

George's mom smiled. "I hope so. Most stories have happy endings. That's what people like. They don't like stories that make them feel bad or confused or unsure. They want to know that everything turns out

---

27. Barry says: I don't understand why she's saying this. In *Unedited*, there's a very good reason for George's mom to be so interested in characters from books. But here . . . ?

28. *** replies: They're just having a conversation. It's meta-fiction. Don't worry about it.

well in the end. When they don't get that assurance, they turn against the book. If the book made them feel bad, they assume the book itself must be bad."

"Are you saying people are stupid?"

She had never had any but the kindest words for human beings. George never imagined he would hear his mother disparage anyone. She burst out laughing. "God, no!" she exclaimed, meeting his expectations and realigning his understanding of her. "They're not stupid. People just have expectations, and when those expectations aren't met, they're disappointed. See?"

"I guess."

George didn't see. The conversation had diverged from George's original intention, which had been to assess what he and Mike might encounter should they actually succeed in this mad quest to find Barry Lyga. Or Gayl Rybar. Or both of them. But then his mother took George's hands in her own.

"Everything changes in stories, George. Sometimes when you least expect it, everything changes. In the end, I would tell any character to keep trying for her own happy ending, to keep fighting. So she never surrenders. So she never gives up."

CHAPTER 16

Mike was ready to give up.

Blind, he stumbled forward, arms extended, feeling his way in the pitch black, begging himself not to panic. The corridor turned left, then right, then left again, then seemed to double back on itself. Mike was lost. *Him.* The budding architect who couldn't remember the goddamn floor plan.

How had he gotten here? How had he ended up lost in the grim, dark, latter-day underworld that was the subway system's maintenance tunnels?

Something about meeting George on one of the platforms . . . George had called him, excited and excitable. They were to meet. George said he'd found an answer, "You know what I mean?" And for the first time, Mike wasn't entirely sure exactly *what* George meant.

But he went anyway. And now he was lost.[29]

Finally, he came upon a door. Bracing himself (for he had no idea what would be on the other side), he twisted the knob and pulled. Nothing. Pushed. Still nothing. He tumbled out of the corridor onto what he imagined was a subway platform, his eyes not yet adjusted, but perceiving a somewhat familiar blur of concrete pad and turnstile

---

29. The full story of how and why Mike ends up lost in the subway system is recounted in—say it with me, folks—*Unedited.*

gate . . . and he fell to the ground, the light searing his eyes, one hand held up to shield them, as footsteps neared.

"Mike? Mike?"

It was George. He heaved a sigh of relief.

"George!"

Hands were on him . . . larger hands than George's. Someone helped him up, and he leaned into the person, grateful to have emerged from the underworld of the subway system, even if only to a station. As his eyes adjusted, he looked around wildly, but there was only George . . . and a random man.

Well, not really. It was obviously the man who had gotten to Mike first and helped him to his feet, the man who now grinned at Mike lazily. He looked vaguely like a grown-up version of Seth—the football player whom George insisted Mike meet at the dance where everything changed—and in that brief moment, Mike no longer felt afraid . . . because Mike's universe had finally achieved a semblance of clarity about something outside himself.

"You're Gayl Rybar, aren't you?" Mike asked.

The man—for, yes, Gayl was a man, not a woman—nodded and returned Mike's smile. "Indeed I am. You ready to go?"

Ready to go? Was Mike ready to go?

Go where?

Mike was no longer afraid, but he was having trouble catching his breath. He couldn't seem to focus. He'd planned to meet George after they had parted yesterday. And now (or then) he was here. But where was "here"?

Gayl Rybar snickered.

"Give him a second," George said protectively.

Gayl fell silent. George threw a brotherly arm over Mike's shoulders. And that reminded Mike of the plan—or rather, the *quest*, which was for love, for love and for a chance to fix a world so badly broken, a world where Mike and Phil *shared* love.

"Go where?" Mike managed, looking up into Gayl Rybar's eyes.

Something in the older man's eyes shifted then, and he clucked his tongue lightly, not as a tsk or a shaming, but rather as though the action could tip almost-spoken words back down his throat.

"We're in no hurry," Gayl said kindly. "Let's take a moment." And he pointed to the ceiling.

The three of them emerged into the waning heat of the desert, at the same spot where Mike had emerged within sight of Crimson Rocks. George, not a marine, humped a large drab olive pack with the ease of a school knapsack.

Mike watched as George quickly, efficiently, expertly laid out a stack of kindling and wood, then set the whole thing ablaze against the coming desert cold. After a moment, he realized that Gayl was watching him watch.

"What's your deal?" Mike asked pointedly. "We're two kids on an adventure. Do you come along with all of your fans when they ask?"

Gayl chuckled. "Once George said the name *Barry Lyga*, that's all I needed to hear."

He settled cross-legged by the fire and said no more, as though his mere presence would be enough to attract the other two. And it was, for within moments, Mike and George joined him at the fire.

For a long while, it seemed as though night would never fall. They were back in the desert. The sun had completed its journey, but night in the desert always came slow.

Gayl was a writer, yes, but part shaman, too, it seemed. His eyes held secrets. His cadence was lyrical, but grounded.

He told them of his younger years. College. Stumbling upon the words and the works of Barry Lyga in the university library: *Inframan. American Sun. For Love of the Madman.* All the others.

But especially *Inframan.* The book that captivated Gayl, known then online as *gaylwriter*, a pretentious and forward-thinking nom-de-digital. The book that propelled him into his own career.

"I always wanted to meet him," Gayl told them, "but by the time I was a published author, he was dead. Do you boys know the story of *Inframan?*"

With this, as though believing himself a wizard, he produced a copy of the book from under his jacket. If he expected them to be impressed by his mundane conjuration, he was quickly disappointed.

"The basics. From Wikinformation."

Gayl flipped through the book. "I edited that entry. It's mostly right.

So . . ." He closed the book and tucked it away. "There was a Mike Grayson in *Inframan* and now there's a Mike Grayson in the real world. Your turn."

George already knew Mike's story, but Gayl did not. So Mike told the story again, in such a way that it took little time, struggling to connect all the alternate edits he'd inflicted upon the world. He began with the dress of either teal or red, depending, and continued on to other edits—the bathroom brawl/not-brawl with *him*, and then the others, the ones that had happened as though in interstitial, liminal spaces so slender as to be invisible, the ones that had happened, perhaps, in some other place.

The ones that had brought him to this pass. To a world in which he had never been with Phil and she never with him, though he remembered both desperately and passionately.

Gayl nodded sagely throughout, occasionally clucking his tongue in an almost musical fashion, his heavy-lidded eyes projecting that he had heard this story—or one like it—before, but never interrupting. At the conclusion of Mike's tale, Gayl leaned in.

"Wanna hear my story?" Gayl asked.

Mike nodded furiously.

"God, I loved this girl!" Gayl exclaimed.

George burst out laughing, the spell broken. But Gayl shook his head.

"I'm serious. It was that teenage kind of love . . ." He broke off. "No offense. I'm just saying. It was that love you can only have when you're a teenager. I was something of an outcast in high school. I only had two friends, really—a guy and a girl, the charter members of the chess club." He glanced up and smirked. "We were the *only* members. The three of us all alone in a classroom after school, playing chess against one another while our teacher/chaperone watched and graded papers . . . Anyway, they were my two best friends, really. I'd known him since elementary school, and I'd known her even longer, back to kindergarten. He was such a geek and a nerd that even I was ashamed to be around him half the time, but what could I do? He was my friend, right? The only one who'd have me. And she—"

"She was your first love," George interrupted.

Gayl elbowed George in the side. "Excuse me? Who's telling this story?"

George rolled his eyes and scooted away.

"So this girl," Gayl continued. "When I was a kid, I used to wonder if somehow girls were just born with this innate understanding of . . . of girl things. You know? Like makeup and braiding hair and things like that. I thought they must just understand those things innately. Because I never saw anyone teaching them, you know? So I figured . . . Anyway, the girl in the chess club . . . If girls innately understood these things, then she was some kind of mutant girl who was missing that gene. Her hair was always disheveled and greasy. She had these huge glasses that took up half her face, and she always wore baggy jeans and men's shirts."

Here, Gayl paused. Mike wasn't sure why. He wanted Gayl to continue.

"But something happened—I can't remember what; it was so long ago—that put me on the radar of the popular kids. Of the whole school, really. One day I was just another schlub in chess club (though the least schlubby of them, to be sure), and the next everyone was talking about me and I was hanging out with the football team and the cheerleaders, and then the most amazing thing happened: The hottest, most popular girl in school started calling me. Started coming to my house. Even kissed me. It was amazing. Of course, this whole time I was getting so caught up in my newfound fame that I ignored the chess club and my two friends. Stopped taking their calls. Just didn't have time. Forgot to fill out the paperwork to have the club renewed for another school year. I had bigger and better things to do."

George groaned. "Wait, wait, wait," he said. "Let me guess. You found out that the hot girl wasn't really into you. She was just using you to get back at a boyfriend or something. And your new friends turned out not to be real friends. So you went back to the chess club and you apologized to your friends, and then when she washed her hair and took off her glasses, you realized Chess Club Girl was really hot, and she became your girlfriend for real. Right?"

Gayl tilted his head and flashed a wry smile, tinged with regret. "Well, George, no. Here's what happened: My best friend spit in my face. He told me he hated me. And the girl? When I confessed my love to her, she told me I'd hurt her too much to even think about me that way. So when I came back for my senior year, I was completely friendless." Gayl's eyes grew distant. "And it was the most miserable time of my life."

Mike waited for more.

So did George. They exchanged a puzzled glance.

"That . . . That's a terrible story!" Mike finally said. "Who would want to hear that story? Who would want to *tell* that story?"

Gayl shrugged. "I would. It's true and it's real, and sometimes people need to hear the stories where things don't work out well."

"I'm with Mike," George grumbled.

"What was her name?" Mike asked. "The girl who couldn't be yours?"

"Phil," Mike knew Gayl would say in the instant before Gayl actually said it. "But that was her nickname. Her full name was—"

"Philomel," Mike said.

Gayl tilted his head. "No. Philomena. Like the saint."

"Whiskey Tango Foxtrot," George said.

"Was her hair blue?" Mike asked.

Gayl laughed too loudly into the desert dark. "Blue? No. I wasn't into the punk scene. She was a blond. I'm sorry if that's not exotic enough for you, my friend."

Mike ground his teeth in frustration, wondering if he should bother explaining that *he* wasn't into the punk scene either, that Phil's blue tresses were natural, wondering if it was worth even discussing.

"I guess it doesn't matter," Mike said at last, though the idea of claiming that anything Phil-related did not matter rankled him. This was all about Phil. Every detail of Phil mattered. "It's close to the same thing with me. Broke up with her. Probably shouldn't have. *Definitely* shouldn't have. And now . . . We're both in similar situations, though. It's a hell of a—" He bit down before he could say "coincidence."

"Let me tell you my theory," Gayl said. "It's going to sound sort of crazy, but hear me out, all right?"

Both George and Mike nodded.

"I want to talk about how the universe works," Gayl began, and Mike huffed a laugh and said, "You're assuming the universe *does* work," which prompted from Gayl a sad, acknowledging smile as the author retrieved his well-read, beaten copy of *Inframan.*

"Are we getting homework?" George asked with something caught halfway between boredom and terror.

"No. I just want to illustrate a point. Look." He fanned the book open, allowing leaves to fall in dull sequence, words rushing by like a corner-flip animation. "Pages, right? You can't do this with an e-book. You can't fan like this. So you miss out on the basic structure of the book—they can mimic pages on a screen, reproducing length and height, but they can't reproduce that third dimension, depth.

"Now, how do we believe the universe works? The universe moves in one direction, right? It moves forward." Gayl held up a hand to stop Mike, who was about to interject. "Wait. Let me finish. Each second exists in the present moment, right? And we experience that second and then it becomes the past as we move into the *next* second, which is now the present for as long as it lasts before *it* passes us by and transforms into history, and so on and so on."

Now Gayl held the book so that it faced open to Mike and George, the title page showing. Mike could make out:

INFRAMAN

or,

The Coming of the Unpotent God

a novel

by Barry Lyga

"Now watch," Gayl said, turning that page. "A second goes by. That page, that second, is now in the past. And another." He turned another page. "And another." And another. "Each page is thin, two-dimensional, until you stack enough of them together in sequence that you get something multidimensional. We get to look at all of the pages, but only one at a time. And while we're looking at one, we can't perceive the others. We're aware of their existence, but not of their content. This is the structure of the universe. It's the way reality works. Imagine Heaven is just another set of pages, buried deep in the back of the book of your life. You can sense it there because of the book's heft, but that's all. You don't know what's written on those pages and you won't know until you get there. And if you skip ahead to look, it won't necessarily make any sense because you haven't read the pages leading up to it."

It made a strange sort of sense to Mike: he imagined each second as an almost-dimensionless thickness of paper, then an endless number of seconds piling up. It was, he thought—and he knew Gayl thought as well—the fundamental structure of the universe: moments, pages, seconds, particles, call them what you will. Piling paper on top of paper. This was how books are created, but it was also, Mike saw now, how reality was created—one dimension, one layer of reality at a time. "You can look at any single page or moment," Mike said, "and you'll comprehend it, but you won't really understand it until you look at *all* of the pages, in the right order. Otherwise, you lack context."

Gayl shut the book triumphantly. "Exactly. Time is the fourth dimension, moving in one direction. Paging through a book is analogous—it's the time travel aspect of writing. But in your case, you gained the ability to . . ." He riffled the pages randomly, shuffling them back and forth, flipping willy-nilly through the book without even looking at the text.

"You're saying the universe is a book?" George asked doubtfully.

"I'm saying more than that," Gayl pressed on. "Are you guys familiar with fractals? A fractal is a mathematical construct that looks the same on the microscopic level as it does on the macroscopic level. Every time you cut a fractal into pieces, each piece is identical to the original, only smaller. You use an equation to generate them, and the equation undergoes a sort of recursive iteration."

Mike blinked. George shook his head. "Dude, you're talking to two guys who hated calculus."

Gayl shrugged. "Me, too. But my brother Liam is a math genius and he explained it all to me. The equation is repeated over and over, but each time there's a tiny difference to it that jogs the end result. Sound familiar?"

Mike nodded. "That's what's happening when I edit. I kept doing the same thing over and over, but was getting different results."

"Right. Because there's something called 'sensitive dependence on initial conditions.' Which basically means that the outcome of a fractal equation is predetermined based on how it started. You started things not in a relationship with Phil; that's the initial condition, and everything that proceeds from it is affected as a result. The entire universe has a fractal structure. If you took our world, our reality, and started cutting it in half, then in half again, eventually you'd get millions of identical copies of it. And you know what I think they'd look like?" He didn't wait for an answer, but instead simply held up the book again. "I think that *Inframan* is an example of fractal mathematics at work. The kabbalists believe that God encoded the keys to the universe into the Torah; this isn't the Torah, but it's a microcosm of reality, and the keys to our universe are encoded in here. It's Lyga's clue to us, the clue that he's more than just a writer."

"What are you saying?"

"I'm saying that all the things we think are coincidences, all the similarities, are nothing of the sort. They're deliberate. They're encoded into the structure of our universe." Here he brandished *Inframan* triumphantly, as if the book contained all of the answers.

"And a book is the structure of our universe?"

"Not just *a* book. Not just *any* book: a book written by Barry Lyga. *Inframan* is the clue. It's a fractal representation of our entire universe, hence the repetition of the name Mike Grayson, the reappearance of the Inframan character, the recycling of ideas and tropes. It's all the same. Our universe *is* a book, a novel to be precise. There may be more pages beyond this novel—I suspect there may be infinite pages—but for us, our universe is circumscribed by the narrative we belong to. For most people, a book is accessed in a specific manner—reading one page at a time, starting with page one, chapter one, and working through to the end. But for you, Mike . . . for the namesake of the lead in *Inframan*, the universe is randomly accessible. You were able to go backwards in our book and—more importantly—change things. Editing reality."

"So you're saying we're just what, characters in a novel? Like in *Inframan*?"

"*Exactly* like in *Inframan*," Gayl crowed. "Do you guys know what gematria is?" At both shaken heads, he went on. "It's an old kabbalistic practice, a Hebrew sort of alphanumeric mysticism that teaches that when you mix up letters, you can reveal secrets encoded in the holy scriptures. They say that you can even reveal the name of God. Well, you did it, George." Gayl chuckled and flashed George an ecstatic grin. "You did what millennia of kabbalists couldn't do: You deciphered the name of God. My name, anagrammed: Barry Lyga."

Gayl slapped the book shut, causing George and Mike to jump. "Barry Lyga is God!"

Silence descended over the fire. The enormity of it clashed with the insanity of it.

Enormity won out.

"Dude, what are you going to say to him?" George asked. "When we meet him, you know what I mean?"

It took Mike a second to realize George was talking to *him*. "Who? Barry Lyga?"

"Yeah."

"I sort of want to yell at him. I want to tell him he's a shitty writer and he's tormenting me for no reason. But you know what? I'm just gonna ask him to fix things. To fix the world. To put me back together with Phil. That's all."

"What if he says no?"

Mike looked to Gayl Rybar for an answer. But the man who'd pulled him out of the darkness and brought him here wasn't paying attention. Instead, he was reading *Inframan* by Barry Lyga.

Mike's jaw tightened.

They had both had and lost a Phil. In the fractal collision that was reality, it could not be a coincidence. They'd both had love stripped from them.

Phil was the reason behind and for all of this. She was the alpha and the omega. Mike knew that now.

Mike gestured for Gayl's attention and summoned the man's copy of *Inframan* with a crooked finger. Once it was in his hands, he stroked its cover lightly before tossing it into the fire.

Gayl seemed nonplussed rather than outraged.

"If he says no," Mike said, "then God had better hope that *God* has someone to pray to."

"That sounds super aggro and impressive," George admitted, "but you still have to find the guy, you know what I mean? He's God, for all intents and purposes. He could be anywhere on earth. Or off of it."

"He's here," Gayl said with absolute confidence as they watched the book smolder, then burn. "And more to the point, Mike knows where."

Mike goggled. "I do?"

"The Mike Grayson of *Inframan* found Barry Lyga's hiding spot. So that means our Mike Grayson can, too. What have you been unable to stop thinking of?" Gayl asked. "What has obsessed you?"

"Don't say *Phil*," George interrupted just as Mike's teeth occluded his lower lip to produce the first sound in her name.

And Mike realized. Of course. It was the only possibility.

"The underwater hotel," he said.

Gayl nodded as though he'd expected precisely that answer. "Good thing I know where to find one," he said.

¡CLOUD HACK SUCCESSFUL!

**Downloading contents of iMessage chat between
AUTHOR (Barry Lyga) and EDITOR**

LYGA: I know I've said some impolitic things about some of your edits, but I wanted you to know that I really like the paragraph you wrote to open Chapter 17. Lovely stuff.

EDITOR: Sorry, I have to take this call.

CHAPTER 17

Every desert has an oasis. Or should. Actually, Mike had no idea if that was true. He knew very little about deserts. But smack in the middle of the desert outside the city with no name, there was a tiny lake. A causeway led to a small one-story edifice . . . clearly a lobby. Its glass doors beckoned. He could see through those doors. But the surface of this lake glistened in a way that made it impossible to see below the surface.

Mike wasn't sure what to feel. This didn't match his plans. He wondered if his architecture professor had spared him the fact that *there was a fucking underwater hotel right outside the city where Mike had lived his entire life*. Or maybe the story was out of control and someone else was editing now and nothing was hanging together. In the end, it didn't matter. They were here. *It* was here.

The walk across the causeway took less than ten seconds. Neither Gayl nor George tried to catch a glimpse of what lay at the bottom of the lake, so Mike thought it would be poor form if he did.

The doors swished open; the lobby was dim and cool, silent but for the hum of some impressively long-lived, still-running air-conditioning unit. It was like an everted doughnut, an anti-doughnut, with empty space ringing a central column. Leather chairs and sofas clustered around coffee tables covered with magazines. In the center of the lobby—at the central column—was a U-shaped marble counter, over which hung a gilt sign reading WELCOME, below which depended a smaller but no less gilded sign that read RECEPTION. It was deserted. As Mike circled it, trailed by Gayl and George, he saw that built into the other side of the column was a pair of elevator doors.

"Wow." Mike's voice was hushed. "This is like . . . I don't know."

A voice spoke from hidden speakers: "Welcome to AquaSpire! This express elevator will take you to down to the world-famous observation room."

George pushed the Down button before Mike could protest.

In they went. Mike's stomach lurched as they plunged downward. Within seconds, the elevator gently glided to a halt. Cautiously, Mike stepped out. George and Gayl followed just as the elevator door slid shut, and Mike's heart sank at the sound of the car ascending rapidly. He knew that the elevator system had been designed intentionally so, sending the express right back up to the lobby to pick up another cargo of tourist sightseers. The air here felt weird, though. It smelled weird. (Not like chocolate syrup, fortunately.) It was electrically charged and hot, as though something massive and slow was approaching . . . It felt like the impossible.

"Do you feel that?" he asked.

"Do you hear that?" Gayl responded, his head cocked.

"It's rain," George said, articulating Mike's impossible thought.

"It sounds like rain and e. e. cummings," Gayl said.

Mike whirled toward him. "What do you mean?"

Gayl blinked in confusion. "I'm not sure."

The three inched forward toward the observation room, clustered together, suddenly terrified for no reason that Mike could understand. Through an arched doorway, they came upon a dome of perfect, crystal-clear glass, through which translucent blue-green water wafted and swelled. Fish darted all around them. It was precisely as Mike had envisioned it, even with the curvature of the dome, physics be damned.

In the center of the room was a comfortable-looking easy chair in which sat a very familiar-looking man . . . a man Mike sort of, kind of knew from his dreams and Google and all the rest of it.

"Oh," Mike said. "Oh my God."

"That's about right," I said.

Yes, "I." I, watching them all. Describing them all to the best of my ability, discovering them, often, as I go along. Sometimes—and this is true, I swear it—my fingers know the truth of a story or of a character before my mind does; the keyboard is the birthing chamber, the brain merely the . . . the . . . pediatric unit.

That didn't work. That was a shitty metaphor. Sorry.

But the point stands: My fingers type things sometimes before I am consciously aware of them. My fingers invoke plot twists. My fingers know it worked.

So I put them in an elevator. And it started to rain while they descended, even though they were below water at that point, purely because I like the sound of rain and *she* likes the sound of the rain, too. She texted me one night and said, *come lie in bed with me and listen to the rain*. And yes, it sounds like rain and e. e. cummings right now, even as I'm typing these words in a garden apartment in Brooklyn, and even though this is taking place in an environment where rain is impossible.

Why is it raining in real life just when I need rain in the novel? I don't know. I don't think I want to know.

Anyway. They all came in. Mike and George and Gayl.

And now you can turn the page for the next chapter.

¡CLOUD HACK SUCCESSFUL!

Downloading contents of email between
AUTHOR (Barry Lyga) and EDITOR

FROM: Barry Lyga
TO: *** *********
SUBJECT: The Other City and the Underwater Hotel

I'm trying to understand your thinking here. In *Unedited*, Mike and George and Gayl and Joe Roberts (who you just disappeared like an Orwellian unperson) undertake a perilous quest to the Other City in order to find God. It's a harrowing ordeal and there's lots of world-building and character work done there.

But here . . . you're suggesting they just find God pretty easily. And you've removed the Other City entirely, replacing it with Mike's dream of an underwater hotel? Really? We lose SO MUCH! The journey on the subway under the desert . . . Not to mention the Electrostatic Man! George's crucial confrontation on the outskirts of the Other City! The legend of Lucky Sevens and the mystery of the Department of Homeland Statistics . . . So much is lost!

Help me understand your thinking here.

FROM: *** *********
TO: Barry Lyga
SUBJECT: RE: The Other City and the Underwater Hotel

For the last time: *Unedited* will be published, exactly as you intended it. Readers will be able to go there and see every last word you wrote, including the Other City and Joe Roberts.

iCLOUD HACK SUCCESSFUL!

**Downloading contents of iMessage chat between
AUTHOR (Barry Lyga) and AUTHOR'S WIFE (Morgan Baden)**

LYGA: I can't believe I agreed to do this. He's cutting everything that matters. No Global War B. No Monika Seymore and her novels. No Cult of the One Book!

BADEN: You knew they were going to cut things when you signed the contract. I'm sorry it's bothering you this much.

LYGA: I hope no one reads this goddamn thing.

CHAPTER 18

They said nothing for an extended silence, so I said nothing as well.

"You're him," Mike said at last. "Right in front of us. You're Barry Lyga, aren't you?"

I shrugged and stood. The chair disappeared, mainly because I didn't feel like describing it in detail. "You could say I'm Barry Lyga," I told him, "but it's more accurate to say that I'm a version of Barry Lyga. An iteration. More like an avatar of a Hindu god than the god itself."[30]

"I burned your book. I'm not afraid of you."

"People who burn books are always afraid of something, Mike." I nodded toward three pairs of double doors I also don't feel like describing. "Choose your path," I told him. "You have to go alone. Your friends must go alone, too."

Mike's eyes roved over each doorway.

I knew what he wanted. He wanted the door that would bring him back to Phil. I knew, of course, what else he was thinking . . . that this was like the novel *Inframan*, that in the Real World he could have an opportunity to write the ending and to fix his own tragic edits.

"One of these doors leads to the real you, doesn't it?" he asked, predictably. "One of them takes me to the Real World, out of the book, into reality."

---

30. An inexact simile, to be sure, but I think you get the point.

"There is no right path," I told him. "There's no right door. There's just the door you pick and the consequences of it."

"Mike," Gayl said, "we should think about . . ."

But before anyone could stop him, Mike was already turning a doorknob. "You heard him. He was just a *version*. I want the real deal. So I can get to Phil."

Mike's doors opened into a teen's messy bedroom. Picto-novels were scattered everywhere, as well as sheets of paper torn from notepads and sketchbooks. Unlike in most versions of his own bedroom, the sketches and drawings were of people, not buildings.

"Guys," he said, turning back to the door, "this doesn't make any sense—" And he broke off when he realized that the door behind him no longer led to the AquaSpire, but, rather, to what appeared to be a short, dark corridor.

"What the hell?" he asked no one in particular.

A complete circuit of the room revealed no other door, only a small-ish window set high in the far wall that made Mike realize that he was not in a bedroom, but in a basement. There was a desk against the wall to his left, every last inch of its surface covered with an ancient computer and more artwork. Mike ran a hand over the keyboard and mouse. Should he boot it up? He thought back to what he'd read on the Wikinformation page about *Inframan* and about what Gayl had told him of the book. Could this be the Real World? Could it be Barry Lyga's room? Did Barry Lyga create his stories on this very computer—

"Nothing on the computer will help you," a voice said, and Mike jumped back from the keyboard, spinning around to see a girl in the doorway.

He knew this girl. Didn't he? The black hair, the slender frame, the goth look . . .

"Angia Eiphon?" he whispered.

She flashed a smile. It was cold, darker than her black hair and her black eyes. "If you like. But not Phil."

She stepped toward him and the black spots of her eyes faded, leaving only the white, which surrounded him as he shouted, as though in a dream, "PHIL!"

Gayl pushed open the door and took one step over the threshold, then hesitated, desperate to turn and look over his shoulder for the reassurance of his companions doing the same, but stopped dead, caught in the liminal space between one world and the other, straddling the threshold between the underwater world of the AquaSpire and some suburban nighttime sprawl.

I've crossed into another story, he thought. *Like at the end of* Inframan, *when the main characters all end up in different short stories.*

The night was brisk, but not too cold for even his desert-appropriate clothing, and the grass tickled his bare calves. He drew in another breath, savoring the unspoiled taste of the air.

He turned suddenly. He couldn't believe his eyes.

Before him stood Phil, as she would be—he knew—as an adult. The wounded and brilliant and caring and angry teenage girl he'd known and rejected and longed for still lived in her gaze, but she was older, more mature. She had grown, as he had.

On some level, Gayl knew he was being manipulated, knew that he was being granted this vision of Phil not for any sort of altruistic or charitable reason, but rather because it served some dramatic beat in the larger fictive rhythm of whatever narrative Barry Lyga imagined himself concocting. He choked out her name.

"I won't fade away," she said dryly.

"Is it really you?" he asked.

"It's me," she said. "Who else would it be?"

Gayl had resisted as best he could, dedicated and devoted to the prospect of foiling Barry Lyga's plans and intentions . . . but this sudden proximity to Phil (whom he'd believed lost forever) proved stronger than his dedication, stronger than his devotion, and he lunged at her, sweeping her into his arms.

"You're real," he whispered. "You're back."

She shook her head. "Not for you. Someone else needs to talk to you. You have to turn around."

"But I don't—"

"Turn around."

He pulled away from Phil.

He turned suddenly.

He couldn't believe his eyes.

Gayl could not understand how, but he now had a different understanding of the universe, his consciousness raised and opened in ways hitherto unimagined. He'd heard over and over from drug-familiar friends that a general widening of consciousness, a new way of seeing the universe, was typically a part of the drug experience. Here, he faced the same mind-opening experience sans drugs of any sort, as he perceived reality in a whole new way.

"What are you?" he asked.

"Yeah, I got that part. But you're different from me, aren't you?"

"Panel borders?"

Just then, Gayl felt something pressed into his hands. He looked down and saw a brand-new copy of *Inframan*, crisp and perfect as the day it came off the presses back in 1994.

"Why are you giving me this?" Some deep and ineffable part of him, though, knew, for in the moment he held the book, it seemed grafted to him, as though it were a part of him and had always been a part of him, as though he'd lost a limb and now had it replaced not by a cybernetic or bionic prosthesis but rather—miraculously—by the original limb itself.

Gayl's turmoil regarding this sensation was enormous. He did not *want* to want or need *Inframan* in his life. He despised it now and suddenly with a true apostate's disdain. And yet he simultaneously yearned for the book. Despite what he'd learned about its creator (or, more accurately, about the creator of its creator), the book still held the deed to a large and significant swath of his adult life, its influences on him both microscopic and macroscopic, writ large and small. He could remember the first time he'd seen it, spine-out on a bookshelf in one of his college's many libraries, its letters worn not by touch or manipulation but, rather, by years of neglectful repose in the direct path of a beam of sunlight.

He opened his new copy now, and it creaked the same way, as if this could somehow be that same initial copy he'd seen and opened and read voraciously in college.

"No." It hadn't. Gayl had taken to *Inframan* with the complex and simple worship of a true zealot, unable to speak of anything but that novel for days—weeks—after reading it, consistently surprised to find that none of his friends (even among the English majors) had read it or even heard of it, that even his professors regarded him quizzically and with benign ignorance when he essayed the topic of the novel and its author. *Inframan* had been born into the world like a child left in the wilderness, raised by wolves or apes or whatever old pulp-fiction/B-movie cliché one preferred: the child undeniably lives and breathes, but no one knows or cares.

That was true. While Gayl could not think of himself as a "success" *per se*, the fact remained that his books sold well enough and had reached a wide enough audience that his publisher continued to buy new ones from him. Each book made it possible for him to publish the next. He was asked to speak at conferences, to visit schools and libraries, to (occasionally) pen essays or short stories for anthologies—all activities that his research indicated had never been offered to Barry Lyga.

Gayl looked down at the book in his hands, open to the title page:

INFRAMAN

or,

The Coming of the Unpotent God

a novel

by Barry Lyga

"I want to think so," Gayl said. "I really do. But there's so much more that I want to . . ." He trailed off, aware of Phil watching him, aware of the stranger from another universe, aware that he had almost revealed his deepest, most closely held secret: That his ambitions had long ago outstripped his meager talents. That he would never possess the psychological and intellectual gear requisite to climb the mountains he'd put before himself. A familiar sensation swaddled him like heavy fog, and Gayl thought that he would drop to his knees. The sensation was that of failure, of abject and utter failure. And yet . . . when struck by this arrow of failure, when wrapped in its smothering blanket, he had only one defense, which he employed now almost instinctively: an email, received two years earlier, written by someone claiming to be a fifteen-year-old boy ("claiming" because any electronic communication is effectively anonymous and, therefore, unprovable), saying:

> ok so i recintly got your book and i belive you have saved me. i am like yor chartacers,i get picked on evry day,never had a girlfrend. i was almost to the pont of killing myself when i started to read this. what this book has done is shown me that.. hey maby my life isint so bad. maby i do have hope.
>
> you have no idea how much this book changed my life

Gayl had written back, of course, though the details of his response were lost to him. Surely he'd said something to the effect of hoping that the young man had sought help for his depression and was now doing better. But one thing he knew he had *not* said in the reply email was this: That as much as Gayl had changed the boy's life, the boy had changed Gayl's. That he had written to Gayl at a time in his life when Gayl despaired of ever achieving greatness with his writing. The nigh-suicidal boy who'd written to him had saved Gayl in turn, giving him armor to wear against the arrows of failure: no matter what else happened or did not happen in Gayl's life and career, he could always look back to that email and think to himself, *I saved that kid's life.*

And then the strange boy from the other reality was gone, and it was just Gayl and Phil once more, as it had been, as it should have been, as it was. He looked at Phil and could not help smiling, a smile Phil mirrored.

"So, got that out of your system?" she asked, as though his epiphany had been a tantrum.

"Yeah. Yeah, I think so."

"Good. Then you're ready."

His hopeful mien ended her mirroring of him; she pressed her lips into a thin line he knew well from their days together.

"Ready for what's next," she clarified with an unkind tone. "Not ready for us."

"Not yet?"

She shrugged with gravity, not diffidence, a distinction he found himself appreciating. "Not now. Not yet. Maybe not ever. I don't know. You still have a lot to learn, Gayl."

The chill air of the night reclaimed him again. The fire swayed and guttered in the wind, and the air within Gayl went colder.

"What do you mean?" he asked.

Phil's smile went sad. "Look at the book," she said. "I'm here to offer hope. I'm here to sound a note of possibility before what is to come."

He opened the book. A sheet of paper was folded within, and he unfolded it.

And then Phil faded to a slender line topped by a dot, and in a moment of horror, Gayl saw that Phil's silhouette had faded away, the entirety of the world before him nothing more than the white blank of a fresh word processing document. He stepped back, dropping the paper, but it remained before him, standing upright, unfolding itself further now, conjuring new sides and heights and widths as though from nowhere.

"Phil!" Gayl shouted. "Phil! Where are you? Can you hear me?"

He knew she could not. He knew she could not.

He screamed her name again, though, screamed it as he dove into the great white screen of nothing:

"PHIL!"

George passed through the doors and stood in a copse. Somewhere a harmonica played, low, long, mournful.

And he suddenly understood. The music awoke in him a fear and a dread, and he understood that Barry Lyga had no intention of letting them win. He had no intention of letting Mike change the world in order to reestablish his love with Phil.

"You're right," I told him, whispering from the trees. "But consider this, George: you only know this because I'm writing it. Have you thought about what that means?"

George gritted his teeth and spun around. "It means you're not playing fair! It means you're not God—you're the Devil. And it means that we're done playing your game."

He began to run. Faster and faster, the tree branches whipping by, leaves clutching and grasping at him before snapping off with the force of his impact, dying and spinning to the ground in his wake.

"I'm going," George said, running even faster now. "I'm going now. To tell Mike the truth. Out loud."

"Will you find him?" I asked.

"Mike!" George screamed feeling Mike so close. "Mike!"

"MIKE!"

P

H

MIKE

L

phlmk

ie

i.e.

id est

That is to say . . .

I
i want
she is i
not i
i is phil
mike is i
it looks like:

i
i need to go
                                        to i
                to her
                                        to i
                                              and I
                              i w
                          a
                              n
                                    t
to
l
     i
          s
               t
                    e
                         n
                              to
the r   i
               a
                    n
with

you
with i
l   a   r
  o   t   a
      o   t   i
      k   h   n
                            e
    l
       e
           tt
               ers

spilling
it sounds like
rain and
e. e.
cummings
this is i
is him
is her
is us
the world is a page
and we are
letters
making
words
and look and see there are letters there are words that spell
C
    H
    A
    P

CHAPTER 19

Inframan gazed levelly at Mike.

"How did we get here?" Mike asked. *We,* for Gayl and George were with him. They had all stepped through the doors leading out of the room from the underwater hotel and then they were here, in this place. A white, featureless room. And his companions stood still as statues as the little boy who was also Inframan watched, passive and silent.

"What do you want?" Mike balled up his fists, almost unaware he was doing so until Inframan chuckled at the sight.

"Do you think you can hurt me? Do you think you can even touch me? You'll fail at that, as you've failed at everything conceivable to you, everything imaginable."

"I didn't fail to get here," Mike said, now unclenching, then reclenching his fists, as if waking them from sleep.

"True," Inframan mused, and then took a swipe at his ice cream with an impossibly long and narrow tongue. "You made it here, but only with the help of your rather pathetic crew of hangers-on. If you go further, you may not survive. Believe it or not, I'm here to help. I've seen the ending of this tale. It ends with you in a room, alone. More than that, Michael, it ends with a love unrequited. Can you bear that?"

Mike swallowed hard, thinking of Phil, thinking of her gone from him forever. "First of all, why should I believe you? Second of all, who's to say that it can't still be changed? Can't the ending be changed? God could change his mind about how to end things. Maybe I can convince him. That's the whole point of prayer."

Inframan snorted. "How often do you think prayers get answered?"

"Not often," Mike admitted. "Certainly not enough. But it only takes one time."

"You don't understand. You're acting as though this is all still in progress, as though you have the option of changing his mind and getting a new ending. I'm telling you that I've seen the ending already. It's written. You, in a room, alone. Love, unrequited. It's a done deal."

"It's just the ending . . ." Mike stammered. "He wouldn't have to change anything else."

And Inframan became a dragon, an enormous, reptilian hulk, caparisoned in shiny, slick black-gold scales, his double-row-toothed mouth roaring wide and blasting out a noisome wind of bad breath and chocolate syrup. He filled the room; he exceeded the room, yet was contained within the room, though that should have been—was—impossible. He reared his head and clawed the floor with hard, horny nails the size of steak knives and the color of old shoes, the rending and shrieking sound of the floor rattling Mike's teeth, his bones.

"Turn back!" Inframan thundered, his voice as big as his body, crushing the air from the room and from Mike's lungs. "Turn back or be destroyed!" A curl of smoke wisped from Inframan's left nostril, an enormous cavern large enough for Mike to insert his fist without brushing the rim. "I am the darkness of ink and the light of all Creation! I am the God of Failure, and though you have failed to worship me, I forgive you and will devour you in your defeat and in your foundering nonetheless."

Mike squeezed his eyes shut tight and found his breath and his words and spoke: "No."

He heard and felt Inframan shift in the room, that lizardy bulk sinuously twisting and contorting into a new position, and then another roar—more halitotic reek, more chocolate syrup—and flecks of spittle spattering him and the heat of a tongue so close, and he knew Infra-man had leaned into him, his maw gaping so wide that he could devour Mike with but a single snap of the jaws.

"I haven't failed," Mike said. "Not yet. I'm not yours yet. I can still succeed. You haven't won."

The dragon harrumphed, and Mike risked opening an eye, find-ing himself staring directly into one of Inframan's enormous eyes, a yellowish thing with a single black puddle floating at its center, grue-some and unblinking. He longed to put his fist through that eye, to blind the creature, but he knew, even half-blind, Inframan could still destroy him.

"Won?" More smoke curled out from Inframan and wafted to Mike, carrying with it the smell of carrion and chocolate. "You and I aren't in competition; I've been trying to help you. I'm still trying to help you. I'm on your side. Don't you understand?

"*You* caused this, Michael! I tried to stop you. I tried to warn you away from editing reality. Who knows—given enough time, maybe you could have won Phil back the old-fashioned way. You could have grown and changed. And then maybe you could have gone to her and found that there was a place in her heart a bit emptier for your loss, a place she could not merely wall away and forget about. A place she needed open and filled. But no. You were too impatient. You thought you were special. You had power, and you had to use it. Strength became its own end rather than a means. Given the chance, you tried to make things better for yourself, not caring what would happen to anyone else. And so it's your fault the universe is damaged, your fault history's been rewrit-ten and fucked up beyond belief. Phil hates you and it's your fault, and that's it."

It was true; of course it was true. It was true and Mike knew it to be true, and yet he did not care. He had mangled things, bungled things, brought his oldest friend and his newest friend to this pass, yet he was helpless to do anything but fight. To push on. To pursue the dream and the reality of Phil, no matter where or when or how long it took him.

"You can't stop me," Mike said to the dragon. "If I go back now, what happens? I live without Phil. Everyone—including her—thinks I'm some crazy stalker. Maybe I'll get arrested someday and that's how I end up in a room, alone. But none of that is worse than this: not trying. I know—I *remember*—how things were before I messed them up. And I'm not just talking about those edits I made. I messed up before that. With Phil. Maybe we would have been together forever, if not for me. Or maybe if I'd been different, we never would have gotten together in the first place, and that would have been okay. But I screwed it up. I own that. And because I own it, I can never, *never* give up trying to fix it.

"So, sorry, Inframan. I won't stop. I can't stop. I can't live the future you described to me. The worst thing that can happen to me is to be in that room alone." Saying those words, he realized their double meaning, their predictive quality and their reductive power. He laughed, despite the stench of the creature and the closeness of its baleful eye.

"Stop laughing," Inframan growled, turning now to bare his enormous, stained teeth. "Stop it!"

But Mike could not stop. Between gasps, he managed to say, "The worst thing that can happen . . . Oh man! You said it yourself. I can do whatever the hell I want! The worst thing that can happen to me is to be in that room alone!"

"That will happen!" Inframan crowed.

"Right! Would he change the ending to make things worse?"

Inframan, for the first time, had nothing to say.

"I can't die," Mike went on. "You can't eat me or hurt me. The worst thing that can happen to me is that I'll end up in that room alone. So why not go forward? If Barry Lyga isn't going to change my ending, like you said—"

"He might. He might make it worse."

But the dragon's voice, for the first time, trembled with uncertainty. With ironic failure.

"Then maybe he's also willing to change it for the better, not worse. Maybe you don't know everything you think you know. But I'll tell you this much: I won't budge. I'm still not going anywhere. Except forward."

With that, Inframan became the little boy again, his ice cream cone magically replenished. Tears rolled down his cheeks.

"I tried," he whimpered. "I want you to admit that I tried."

Mike knelt before the boy and put a hand on his shoulder. He felt suddenly tremendously paternal toward him, as though he had been there at this child's birth and sworn to protect and love him all his life. If he had had it in his power to give Inframan what he wanted, he surely would have in that moment, swooning to the child's final gambit of fat tears. But Mike knew now what he supposed he'd known all along, from the first moment he'd edited reality: He was powerless. Despite his power, he was powerless, helpless in the face of something greater than himself, of his own love for Phil.

Whether that love had come honestly or not, he could not say. Maybe it had been implanted in him artificially; maybe it was an outgrowth of some mistaken combination of words on a page. But for him, it was real, and it was mightier than anything else in his life. Mightier even than the abrupt love he felt for Inframan.

"You tried," he told the child, and hugged him, careful to avoid crushing the ice cream cone between them.

"I failed," the boy bawled, nestling against Mike's shoulder. "No one likes me and no one loves me and no one will ever love me, even though I never hurt anyone and I just want to help. Really. That's all I want. I tried to help and I failed. I always fail. I always screw up."

"No, you don't," Mike said, comforting him. "No."

"I do! I always do!" he blubbered, then pushed away. Mike anticipated some horrible light in his eyes, horns from his skull, fire from his nostrils, but no—he was still just a little boy, with tremulous brown eyes clouded by tears.

"I always fail!" he raged, and threw down the ice cream cone in a tantrum. He stomped a foot on the floor. "I'm the God of Failure!"

And he vanished, leaving only the melting brown smear of chocolate ice cream on the floor as a reminder that he'd been there.

Still down on one knee, Mike stared at the ice cream until George's voice came to him, saying, "What happened?"

Mike looked around. George and Gayl had come out of their trances, staring at him and at the ice cream.

"Oh," Mike said. "There's a door."

Yes. A door.

Mike stood and opened the door, and they came into my presence.

PART V

CHAPTER 20

I spent some time imagining how I wanted them to come into my presence. I considered some crazy description of an abstract landscape and maybe choirs of singing angels and glowing balls of light in the air. You know, because I'm God and all that. But that seemed like an awful lot of work. Yes, yes, I know—it's just "words on a page," but I don't think you know how much work "words on a page" can be. I would have to design the environment in my mind, then figure out which details mattered. And let's say I decided that those singing angels were a good idea: Well, what are they singing? How loudly? How many of them are there? Will they keep singing during the dialogue scene to follow, and if so, how often should I intrude on the dialogue to point this out? Are they moving around? Interrupting and distracting with their motions?

You can see my dilemma.

In the end, I settled on another plain white room. Boring, yes, but be honest—at this point, you haven't read all this way for the scenery of Heaven. You want to know what happens next. You want to know if I could possibly be so cruel as to leave Mike in a room all alone at the end, if I could be so cruel as to leave a love unrequited.

We're getting there. I promise you. We're so close.

"Is it really you this time?" Mike asked upon seeing me. I was standing in the white room, my hands clasped dramatically behind my back, waiting for him.

"Is it really you?" he demanded. "Because I want the real deal."

"I'm an avatar, Mike. A version of Barry Lyga translated into prose. It has to be this way; trust me. You can't handle the real me."

"It doesn't matter what I can or can't handle. I came here, I fought to get here, to see God. That's what they came for, too." He gestured to his companions, standing slightly behind him, reminding me of body-guards or superheroes, I'm not sure which.

"Mike, haven't you ever read the Bible? Don't you know about God and Moses? God showed his true face to Moses for, like, half a second, and Moses aged a hundred years. Are we really going down that road? Believe me, kid, you couldn't handle seeing the real me."

"Why? Are you that magnificent?"

I laughed. "No, I'm just a guy pushing forty,[31] sitting at his computer. But trust me, you can't handle it."

"I can imagine that; why can't I handle it?"

"Your universe isn't detailed enough. I see the world in high-def; you're stuck in standard."

"I want to see the real you."

I sighed. "Fine. But don't say I didn't warn you."

I showed them the real me, from the real world. To them, it appeared like this:

Barry Lyga stands 5 feet, 10.98351 inches tall when barefoot and standing fully erect. We will begin at the top and work our way down. His head is covered by 101,427 hairs, beginning at a hairline that recedes over the forehead. We begin by choosing, arbitrarily, a hair that is midway equidistant between the tops of his ears (as measured over the curvature of his skull) and midway between the nape of his neck and the lowermost

---

31. Actually, by the time this damn book is published, I'm *fifty*. Which, let me tell you, sucks. Remember way back on page 81, when I had Mike's architecture professor say, "Architecture is an old man's game"? Well, I'm an old man now. The things I dreamed of doing in my youth—my twenties, when I conceived of *Inframan*; my thirties, when I wrote this book—are now possible, but only now that I'm so damn old. And will anyone give a shit about the ramblings of an old man?

jut of his chin, omitting for measurement purposes the perimeter of his
nose and measuring, therefore, directly over his mouth, between his eyes,
and over his forehead. This particular hair is 3.72 inches in length and
0.2 mm thick at the base, tapering to 0.1 mm at its farthest extension. It
was cut approximately three weeks previous to the writing of this paragraph with a Braun electric razor with a number-two razor attachment
at a small barbershop in the lower blocks of Court Street in Brooklyn,
New York.[32] The hair is a reddish brown in color, closely approximating
a tone of CMYK 0-67-98-68, the red portion a recessive genetic trait
from Scottish ancestors[33] that occasionally surfaces, as now. The second
hair is located 0.5 mm to the right of the first, assuming one is observing Lyga's head from the top and behind; this second hair measures 3.75
inches in length and 0.19 mm thick at the base, tapering to 0.11 mm at
its furthest extension. The hair is a deep brown in color, closely approximating a tone of CMYK 0-50-74-70. The third hair is located 0.17 mm
to the right of the first, still assuming one is observing Lyga's head from
the top and behind, this third hair measuring 3.76 inches in length and
0.23 mm thick at the base, tapering to 0.09 mm at its furthest extension.
The hair is a deep brown in color, closely approximating a tone of CMYK
0-51-72-71. The fourth hair . . .

And then I took mercy on them all.

"See?" I asked through my avatar. "Do you understand?"

You—as in *you, the reader*—probably don't really get it, but try to
imagine what it would be like if everything you saw in the world were
presented to you in exacting, exasperating, explicit, and total detail. So
you couldn't just pick up a glass, for example. You would have to burn
through innumerable brain cycles noting the curve of its rim, the thickness at lip and base, the exact clarity, the albedo, the circumference,

32. For simplicity's sake, let us stipulate that—unless otherwise mentioned—all of the hairs on
Lyga's head were cut in such a fashion at such a place by such a gadget at such a time.

33. Lyga is one-eighth Scottish on his mother's mother's side, his maternal grandmother's
mother's maiden name having been MacPherson. She was blessed with red hair and green eyes, and
while interbreeding with Slavic, Germanic, and Mediterranean stock caused brown hair pigmentation
to predominate, the Scottish genes occasionally surface, as now. In other words: sometimes you can
see streaks of red in my hair and beard.

the weight and density and more, all in terms scientific and rote. Every action you take, every twitch, everything you see, taste, touch, smell, hear—*described*.

You'd go crazy, right?

That's what they got a taste of, just then. Mike and the others staggered backward toward the door, their expressions uniformly dazed and worn, as though battered. It was a familiar sensation for poor George, but for the others, it was new and horrible.

"Oh God . . ." Mike said without the slightest trace of irony.

"Now do you get it?" I asked. "This is just a simulation of the real world. You wouldn't be able to comprehend the *real* real world. That's why I have to fake it here on the page. That's why all writers fake it on the page. The real world is too detailed and too intense. And, honestly, too boring for prose. In the real world, we sort of automatically filter out the details that don't matter, but you guys are characters; you're used to living in a world where everything is described, not actually seen. Where everything that is described is important, so you have to pay attention to it. You don't have filters in place to help you figure out what matters and what doesn't, so when writing, I have to use metaphors instead. We don't have metaphors in the real world. We use them, but they don't actually exist. For this bit, I have to just say that I have short brown hair. Otherwise, we could have gone for hundreds of pages just describing my hair." I ran a hand through it. "And I don't even have that much of it left these days!"

They looked at me as though . . . oh, hell, as though they didn't believe me, okay? There's no point prettying it up for you with an analogy or a simile. I think you get it, right?

"Look, guys, writing is about reducing complexity, to a degree. Filtering out the stuff that doesn't matter and committing to paper only the stuff that does. You leave out everything else and let the reader's imagination do the rest of the work. Even for something as simple as: 'The dog ran.' Some readers will imagine the dog's tail wagging for balance, the tongue lolling out to cool it off.[34] Others won't see those

---

34. And now you're probably seeing those details, whether you originally did or not, right?

things, but will see other details. And let's not even talk about breed! I haven't mentioned the breed of the dog, but everyone reading this book is picturing a specific breed or a specific sort of mutt."

"No two people ever read the same book," Gayl whispered. "The words are the same, but the story is always—"

"Stephen King says that stories are telepathy," I told them. "I say they're mind control, but mind control of an imperfect sort. When I write a story I can force you to imagine certain things, but there's always a level of control I can't attain. That is the flaw in storytelling. That's the flaw in creation, period. If what I imagine only communicates to you imperfectly, then how can we imagine that God created the world perfectly? My reality—the 'real world'—is nothing more than the imperfect reflection of God's imagination."

"I thought *you* were God," George said.

I ignored him and went on: "Or maybe it's more accurate to say that stories are time travel. I'm writing these words now, on August 24, 2010.[35] But they're being read a month or a year or ten years from now. Hell, maybe even a hundred years from now. I'm long dead, but the words I'm typing right now are—at the same moment—communicating with someone born after I died."

"So then the nature of story," Gayl said, excited, "isn't just in the mind of the author. It has to do with a sort of collaboration—"

"An uneven, unequal collaboration."

"—between the reader and the author!" Gayl ran a hand through his hair, which wasn't thinning like mine yet, but would be soon. "Wow. Oh, wow, I never thought of it that way!"

"She died; he mourned," I said. "Shortest story in the world. Cause and effect. Action and reaction. Emotion. Two characters. Both of them change by the end. And the reader's imagination fills in all the details. Done and done."

---

35. Actually, I wrote most of this scene much earlier than that and this paragraph in particular was written possibly two years earlier, but August 24, 2010, is the day I sat down to revise this chapter, the day when I decided to add this specific paragraph to this specific exchange, so that's the day I'm using.

"This is all well and good," Mike said, "but I'm not here for some bullshit philosophy lesson. I want to know: Is this really you? This is what you look like?"

"Generally, sure. It's how I would describe myself, at least: Average height, average build. Brown hair and eyes, unshaven, with a chin beard . . . Close enough for government work, as we like to say."

He looked back and forth between Gayl and me. "You guys look a lot alike."

"Well, yeah. We're versions of each other. But, Mike—this isn't what you came here for, is it? You came for the reason all pilgrims visit their gods. You want a boon." I grinned in a manner I hoped was reassuring. Maybe it was, maybe it wasn't. "You all want something from me, don't you?"

They were silent.

"Don't you?"

George shrugged. "I don't want anything," he said very quietly. "Not from you."

Strangely, it was true. I knew, of course, the one thing that George wanted, for I was the one who had given him that impulse and that need and that drive. His two remaining secrets.[36] Moreover, it was entirely in my power to give George the thing he wanted most, and I had considered it, had been considering it for several chapters now. It would require rewriting the ending to the book (I had already written the ending months ago), and I really *really* liked the ending, but . . . if I pulled it off, giving George what he wanted would be a literary coup, a stunning ending that would pull the rung[37] out from under the reader's expectations.

But I decided not to do this. Because it would mean imposing my

---

36. I promise I will tell you before the book is over. Yes, George has three secrets. Unlike Fanboy, the protagonist in my first novel, I won't be keeping his particular "third thing" a secret. Some magic tricks only work once before the audience tires of them.

37. That's a typo, but I decided to leave it in. If you think about it, having a rung pulled out from under you would be just as shocking as having a rug pulled out from under you . . . and lots more dangerous.

will on George, and this is something I was not willing[38] to do. I liked George. Somewhere along the way, he'd grown on me. Mostly in the process of writing *Unedited*, the longer companion to this book. He's a little thin in this one, I admit, but if you read *Unedited* . . . oh, then you'll see George in all his glory!

I'm not sure why he means so much to me; after all, for much of the novel, he's unaware of the progress of the plot, merely another piece on the game board that Mike keeps rearranging with his "editorial powers." And yet, at some point, he became very real to me, and I hated that he was drummed out of the marines, hated that he lost one of the only things he cared about in the world, a goal he'd aimed for his entire life, a goal he'd accrued as his most potent and enduring form of self-identity. Maybe because on some level he reminded me of a friend of mine who, like George, wanted only to protect people, to defend them from enemies and keep them from being hurt, all because no one had been there to shield him when he'd needed it. George was important to me, and I hated what I had done to him and what I would do to him in the future.

But for now, I had to set George aside and move on. To Gayl. My doppelgänger, after a fashion. Gayl was more like me than I cared to admit, just as I often said that *Fanboy* was "more autobiographical than I should admit in public."[39] Gayl was a version of me from many time periods, deconstructed and reconstructed repeatedly until he was almost—but not quite—his own character, hence the scrambled name. He was not a direct analog or avatar of me—he was an iteration. He had his own career that mirrored mine but was different from mine.

"How about you, Gayl? What do you want from me? Surely you

---

38. But wait! I'm the author! I impose my will on *all* of the characters! It's the nature of writing! Hmm . . .

39. That's a line that, when used on panels and at signings, always gets a laugh. It took me a long time before I realized that it was a subconscious modification of something I had written in the unfinished *Inframan* back in college, when a friend of mine comments that my novel *His Darkness* (another never-to-be-written novel by the dead Barry Lyga) was "too autobiographical for your [my] own good." It's strange how something intended as a dark, dramatic, portentous line in one context can become wholly unconsciously revised and restructured, then delivered in another context that makes it comedic.

didn't come here just to provide moral support and the occasional convenient plot explanation?" I grinned because truthfully those were Gayl's primary functions in the story, other than being another in a fun series of ways to both mock and revere myself at once. "You've written versions of my books," I went on, "so you must have some idea of what you can get from me."

Gayl thought slowly and deliberately, just as I knew he would, just as I wanted him to, just as I would in the same situation. "I suppose I could ask for what Mike wants," he said, picking his words carefully.

"Was that your way of asking for something?" I asked him, knowing it wasn't.

"Or I suppose," he went on, ignoring me, knowing that I knew it wasn't, "I could ask you to explain why I exist. Who and what I am. Why you gave me your name. Why you gave me a version of your life and career and books when there was already a version of you in the world."

"I can answer that," I told him.

"But I don't want to know anymore," he said, unsurprisingly. For I had already written a section to use at some point, and now was the time to use it, and Gayl, I had decided, would be my excuse.

"I don't need to know those things anymore. I've learned they don't matter. So I want to know what happened to Barry Lyga," he told me. "I want to know what happened on August 5, 2005, to the Barry Lyga in my universe, the one who wrote *Inframan* and *American Sun* and *Redesigning You* and the others."

"Of course you do," I told him. "And I can show you."

THE DEATH OF
BARRY LYGA

Barry Lyga knew how the story ended.

It was his latest work in progress—*The Gospel According to Jesus*—and given the subject matter, the ending was preordained, perhaps in multiple senses of that word. It would end, as it must, with Jesus on the cross, with a final thought that Barry had kept locked in his imagination for years, ever since the idea of the book had occurred to him. That, he had come to realize, was how he wrote books—he knew the beginning and the ending, and sometimes he knew something of the middle. But usually he started with a blank computer screen, an opening scene or handful of scenes, and an ending to work toward. In the middle was—he hoped—magic.

But there are different kinds of magic, different types. There's the magic of fantasy novels, and there's the magic of the stage, and while he had spent his life fervently searching in his books for the former, he'd found only the latter, more accurately described as "illusion." And illusions may thrill or frighten or illuminate or awe, but in the end all illusions fade. Barry Lyga desperately did not want to fade.

Now, on August 5, 2005, he had come to a horrible crossroads. His latest book had not done well, even by the lax and tolerant standards of his small publishing house (a tiny, four-man operation run from somewhere in Ohio). Each book, he had always said (both aloud to friends and to himself), needed only to supply enough money to his coffers to pay for him to write the next one. He cared not, he claimed, for the *New York Times* bestseller list, nor for awards, nor for any of the other typical and standard metrics of success. He wanted only to keep writing, to have the writing be his life's work, without interruption, and so long as each novel allowed him the financial freedom to write the next, he would be happy.

He convinced himself of this early on. It was not a difficult conceit to swallow.

He had achieved this aim since college, beginning with the publication of *Inframan* and the others, leading up to the publication of *For Love of the Madman*, which had been in stores for only a week thus far, but which showed every sign of failure. Preorders had been "dismal," in the refreshingly honest parlance of his editor, and there had been no early reviews to speak of, save for the occasional mention on a blog or a few half-hearted attempts on AwesomeReads.com. No one was talking about the book. No one was reading the book. And sure as hell was hot, no one was buying the book.

It would be a year before *Sxxxxx Cxxx*, his latest novel, was published, and even if it did spectacularly well (and at this point, seven novels and a short-story collection into his career, what were the odds?), it would be another six months after that before he could count on his first royalty check. He had stripped his lifestyle down to the bone. He ate frugally, adhering to a strict food budget each week. He'd stopped attending movies or sporting events; he did not even rent movies online, preferring instead to wait for the local library to offer the DVDs. He had canceled his internet service, relying instead on a coffee shop some four blocks away, and had sold his car; he walked everywhere he needed to go, taking a bus when absolutely desperate to journey more than a mile or two from his home. He gave up on haircuts as a needless expense, and his hair, though thinner, had become as long as he'd once worn it in college, down to his shoulders.[40]

---

40. I'm not going to lie to you; this whole paragraph makes me extremely uncomfortable. So uncomfortable that I want to cut it . . . but that makes me pretty sure I shouldn't. Because if it make me uncomfortable, doesn't that mean it's powerful? Maybe even true?

And yet despite all this—despite these sacrifices—he still had too little money to last him through the publication of *Sxxxxx Cxxx*, much less to that mythical royalty check.

He was a failure.

At his back, the creature giggled and changed shape. Sometimes it looked like Barry had as a child, always carrying an ice cream cone, perhaps from the now-defunct, long-ago-closed-down Twin Kiss ice cream parlor on Reisterstown Road, where Barry had eaten his first soft-serve ice cream and learned how to love fried potato wedges.

At other times it looked like his father or his ex-girlfriend or the girl who had pulled his pants down on the baseball field in fifth grade, humiliating him.

Sometimes it looked like him, as though an image had pulled itself from the mirror on the wall and decided to walk the world on its own.

But it always sounded the same and it always smelled the same. It smelled like chocolate syrup, like a bottle of Hershey's hooked up to an air compressor and fired straight up the nose.

It always sounded like a dragon.

In high school and in college, he'd been haunted, not by a ghost but by an idea, an idea of failure so large that it was itself a God, the God of Failure, a creature he came to call Inframan.[41] He wrote a novel about Inframan, hoping that doing so would exorcise the idea, purge it from his consciousness, but all it did was make Inframan more powerful. Inframan whispered to him in his sleep, mocked him in his waking hours, tormented him.

He had tried to beat Inframan with words, and in the end, Inframan turned out to be made stronger by words. Every writer, Barry had been told by his acquaintance Art Holcomb, has a million bad words in him, a million words he has to write before he gets to the good ones.

Inframan was those million words times a million writers, then a

---

41. Imagine the horror Barry Lyga experienced when he discovered that comic book genius Alan Moore used the name "Inframan" for a throwaway superhero character in his *1963* comic book, published in 1993, years after Lyga had begun work on *Inframan* the novel. Would people think he had ripped off Moore? he wondered. Would he have to change the title of his opus because of a fucking background character in a comic book?

million more. The very essence of failure, distilled down from a liquid
to a thick, reductive . . .

    . . . syrup . . .

It was time for things to be over, Barry Lyga thought. It was time,
he thought and he knew. It was August 5, 2005. Bifurcation Day. Publication Day. He could no longer exist, this Barry Lyga, this author.
Inframan had to remain on a hard drive, migrating from New Haven
to Owings Mills to Hampstead to Hanover to Las Vegas to New York
to New Jersey, unfinished, like Gayl Rybar's masterpiece. *American Sun*
was nothing more than a file of hasty notes and an idea for yet another
inconclusive ending.[42] The short stories of *The Sunday Letters and Other
Stories* were written but unpublished, ill-suited for publication in any
event. And the other novels? *Emperor of the Mall* and the others? Nothing more than high concepts. Notions. A paragraph of description here.
A character name there. A few fully realized scenes never committed to
paper or pixel, socked away instead in Barry Lyga's subconscious, whence
they occasionally pop up, unbidden, like children given up for adoption
stalking their birth parents.

On August 5, 2005, the phone call comes from a traditional inn in
Japan at 2:00 a.m. local time. It comes from and to another universe,
as another Barry Lyga's agent calls, whispering so as not to awaken the
inn's other guests sleeping behind rice-paper walls, informing him that
Houghton Mifflin Books for Children has won the auction for his first
novel, not the literary opus *Inframan*—an exploration and exploitation
of the nature of textual realities and the relationship between reality and
fiction—but rather *The Astonishing Adventures of Fanboy and Goth Girl*,
a young adult novel about a sarcastic fifteen-year-old outcast (based on
Lyga's own teen self) and the girl of his nightmares, the titular Goth Girl.

Inframan will never be finished. *American Sun* will never begin. And
the Barry Lyga destined to write these books? The iteration of Barry Lyga
who dreamed them and sculpted them to perfection in his mind's eye?

---

42. To be precise, the following sentence: "Cam pulled the trigger and realized that no matter
what did or did not happen next, he had changed the world."

Why, that Barry Lyga can no longer exist. His existence is an impossibility, for even if he someday *were* to write *American Sun*, to finish *Inframan*, to author all the others, they would come later, they would come after *The Astonishing Adventures of Fanboy and Goth Girl*, and they would be not of the Barry Lyga who dreamed them as his career, but of some other Barry Lyga.

And so that first Barry Lyga must—by force of logic, if nothing else—be gone. And if he must be gone, then he was here, and if was here, then he lived. And so he must die.

This was not a difficulty or a complexity for the other Barry Lyga, for the one on the phone with his agent on August 5, 2005. He gave—I gave—no thought at all to the first Barry Lyga. Not a single thought at all. Not a single regret. In college and for years after, he had fantasized himself the author of *Inframan* and the others, and now—in less than a heartbeat—he discarded that dream, that career, that legacy, and that life, condemning the dream iteration of himself to death as he accepted the two-book deal from Houghton Mifflin, unsure at the moment what his second book might be, though the story of an abused boy had been nagging at the back of his brain for years now, and he had an inkling that maybe—maybe—it might be time to tell it. It might be worth his time and the reader's time. Possibly.

There was so much to do. Death was merely an inconvenience, a detail to be ironed out, a *t* to be crossed, an *i* to be dotted.

It's not that he wished to die.

He simply no longer wished to live.

There was another Barry Lyga, he liked to fantasize. A Barry Lyga who had not made these mistakes. Call him, if you like, the Barry Lyga of Earth 2.[43] This Barry Lyga would be a bit older. A bit wiser. Maybe he would have wisely given up the pursuit of publication and would live to a ripe old age, surrounded by loved ones, beloved and content,

---

43. A parallel-worlds nomenclature lifted from the DC Comics of Barry's youth, once quite obscure to a mainstream audience, but now well known due to its use on *The Flash*, a TV show on the CW. (Plug: I wrote a series of novels based on that TV show. Go buy them—they're fun, and I don't show up in them at all!)

having lived and worked in some fulfilling career that this Barry Lyga could scarcely imagine.

Or maybe . . .

"Maybe he just wrote better fucking books," Barry Lyga said aloud to his cramped, empty apartment.

And died.

CHAPTER 21

Funny.[44]

I never intended to write any of that. I never intended to describe my own death. If you want to know the truth, it sort of freaked out my girlfriend at the time that I killed myself off at all.

I couldn't explain to her how liberating it was, how rejuvenating. It wasn't *me* dying; it was a version, an iteration, an avatar. It was a useless chunk of me that I had discarded long ago. It felt good to kill that Barry Lyga. It freed me from him, from his expectations and his needs. I never meant it to be a part of the book. I always intended to leave "his" death a mystery, but then one day it occurred to me how to write it, how to frame it, and I thought that it was very likely that Gayl—Gayl, of course, of all the characters; Gayl the writer; Gayl the me—would want to know how it happened.

In the big book (which, in case you haven't noticed, is how I think of *Unedited*), there was this big mystery about what happened to Barry Lyga in 2005. How he died. Et cetera. I almost cut it from this version entirely, but my editor (you know, good ol' ***) wanted to keep it. And any chance I have to heap derision on myself (in whatever iteration), I'll take it.

---

44. "Funny strange," of course, not "funny ha-ha," the latter of which has been lacking in this book, unless you appreciate the sort of weird, obscure, intellectual and pseudo-intellectual in-jokes that I appreciate. For which I apologize.

"I thought differently," Gayl said as I finished the story. "I thought the wrong things mattered. And I hated people for their success, and I hated myself for not having the same success. You made me in your image, didn't you?"

I said nothing.

"Now you've had your eyes opened," Gayl told Mike. "You've seen how damaged your world is and you've seen who's responsible. A feckless, self-obsessed God. So it's simple, Mike—make your choice. Do you want the world fixed? Or do you just want Phil back?"

"I can't make that decision!" he cried. "How can you expect me to? I'm weak—"

"You're not weak. Not all the time. You've just misapplied your strength. But you've been strong for her, Mike. Think of what you've endured to get her back."

Mike thought for a moment. He remembered his dialogue with Inframan, remembered how his obsession with Phil had led to disaster for him, for her, for the world. He remembered, too, his own ruminations on obsession, how closely it is allied with love, kissing cousins, so easy to mistake one for the other.

And in the end, he nodded to himself, steeled himself.

He said, "I want Phil back. That's what I want, and I know you can do it."

I sighed. "You didn't surprise me, Mike. I was sort of hoping you would. You've been very single-minded throughout, though, so I guess it's not that big of a shock that you're still singing the same old tune."

"You *made* me this way," he countered. "It's not my fault."

"Fair enough. Come with me."

We walked through the door together. Just the two of us. Leaving the others behind. (They have different fates in the big book, if you're interested.)

"I'm going to show you the beginning of the world."

"Oh, really?"

"Watch. Watch. I will show you perfection."

See

?
See

                    what the world

                                        once
was?

Pure
L
  i
  k
   e

     f
      a
          l
           l
      i
       n
       g

        r
        a
                i
                    n

Perfect

Dull

Dead

And then you/me

This world
mar
        ked
            in
                black

Ask yourself:

Are the letters added to the page

Or subtracted from it?

Is this an act of creation

Or of reduction?

Hold
my
hand.

Tight.

We're almost

CHAPTER 22

"Open your eyes, Mike."

I released his hand and watched him.

"Welcome, Michael. Welcome to the Real World."

"Where are we?" he asked.

"This," I told him, "is where I grew up."

We stood in the backyard of the house in Hampstead where I'd grown up—the overgrown woods off to our right, the barbed-wire fence that divided our property from the cow field to the left. A single cow—I don't know what breed; I never cared and I can't be bothered to check now, quite honestly; the damn cow's just there for verisimilitude, okay?—chewed her cud just on the other side of the fence, watching us with dull brown eyes. The sun hung low in the west, melting the clouds along the horizon. It was the best I could do without going back in time and taking a picture.

"I can see all of this," he said. "I can understand it. It's not like before, where there was . . ." He shuddered. "Too much. Of everything."

"Yeah, that's because I lied just now: I'm just faking it again for you. You're not in the real world. The first Mike Grayson, the one from *Inframan*, he got to go to the real world because at the time, I (or the version of Barry Lyga who wrote that novel) didn't really understand what the real world would look like to a fictional character. Or maybe I just changed my mind about how to deal with that. Anyway, it doesn't matter. You're just in a facsimile of reality. There're all kinds of details I'm leaving out because they would just bore people at this point."[45]

"Oh. It seems nice here," he added after a moment.

"I fucking hated it." I turned him around, pointing him at the house. "I hated every last instant in this place. I was moved here after my parents got divorced. Didn't want to go, but I had no choice. This house and this town came to represent everything I wanted to escape in my life. Stupid hick town in the middle of nowhere in the 1980s. Before the internet. We didn't even have cable TV. It was like living in another century. No wonder I read nothing but comic books and science fiction and fantasy. I was trying to escape the only way I knew how—with my brain."

"What does this have to do with Phil?"

"Oh, Mike . . ." I sighed. "It's not about Phil. It never has been."

"It's *all* about Phil!" he protested.

"You don't know what it's about," I chided him. "You have a child's view of romance, a bully's view of love. You want Phil to be a very specific, very constrained person, hemmed in by what works for you, what you need. That's not mature, Mike. And it sure as hell isn't love."

"Fuck you!" he yelled. "I just prioritized her over the goddamn *universe*. Don't tell me I don't love her!"

"Yeah, you love her. In your way. Maybe it'll grow and ripen and mature. I don't know. This'll all be over before then. But don't kid yourself: you didn't prioritize *her* over the universe; you prioritized *yourself*, and your happiness. You prioritize her because of what she does for and to you, not because of what she does to and for herself."

His expression softened the tiniest bit. "I need her to be happy," he said quietly.

"That's a pretty unclear statement. Are you saying that you need for her to be happy herself? Or that you need her in order to be happy?"

45. In the original draft, I listed some of these details, but you know what? I was right! They bored early readers, so I took them out.

"Shit." Mike pondered. "Both . . . ?"

"That's great, but it's putting a hell of a lot on her, don't you think? And again—that's not necessarily love. Could be. Could also just be obsession."

He threw his hands in the air. "I don't care anymore! I have to be honest with you. I just don't care, okay? I didn't come here and do all of this to meet God! I didn't do it to learn the mysteries of the universe! I did it—"

"You did it for her. I know. I understand. You did it because you swore you would do anything to have her back. And I'm here to tell you that it doesn't matter. It doesn't matter what you say, what you think, what you feel. It doesn't matter that you're willing to challenge your God. Because in the end, she doesn't love you. And that's it. Nothing you do or say can or will change that. Grow up. Accept it."

Mike glared at me, then—with defiance—sat on the grass, right on the spot where we buried Spacey, our black Lab/cockapoo mutt. He didn't know he was sitting there, and I didn't tell him.

"Make me," he growled. "Make me accept it. You're God. Make me."

"Stop pouting," I told him. "You're acting like a child."

"Well, so what? You've taken away everything I care about. You're going to leave me in a room, alone, with love unrequited. Why shouldn't I act like a child?"

I held out a hand to him. "Come on. Stand up. Let me tell you my story."

He crossed his arms over his chest. "I don't care about your story."

"Sure you do. You're curious, aren't you? Just a little bit? I made you that way. Let me tell you your first memory."

"What?"

"Your first memory. A neat little trick writers use sometimes, where they have a character think back to the first thing they can remember. You're about to experience yours, mainly because I just came up with it."

And sure enough, despite himself, Mike couldn't help but think of a time when he was four or five years old, a child in kindergarten.

There were large blocks in the room, maybe eight inches long each, made of a light wood. They were stacked against one wall, and while they had always been there, for some reason on this day, Mike became obsessed with them, to the degree that he could not concentrate during the daily recitation of the alphabet, skipping *d* and swapping the positions of *m* and *n*, when usually he could recite the alphabet backward without missing a letter. Not today. Today he had eyes only for the tall wall of blocks that beckoned to him, and he swore that—come playtime—he would attack that wall, tear it down, reduce it to its component parts, then build a truly awesome fort for him and friends to use and play in for playtime. Yes, oh yes, that would happen. Nothing would stop him.

He beelined for the blocks, along with George and two other friends, the plan already disseminated in hushed whispers during naptime. They assailed the wall, tore it down, and began construction of a walled-in square, with an opening on one side for ingress and egress. They had decided on a game of soldiers and jihadists[46], with the jihadists holed up in a bunker (which suspiciously and conveniently resembled a square of large wooden blocks) and the soldiers attacking from without, just like on the Saturday-morning cartoons they watched every week without fail. As they put the finishing touches on the fort, though, their teacher announced that playtime was over, the allotted time having burned through as they labored to build their fort. Grumbling and complaining, George and the others helped Mike reduce the fort to its components once more and then stacked them neatly against the wall, as though they had never moved, never been reconfigured, never been anything more than a stack against the wall.

When Mike's mother came to pick him up that afternoon, the teacher recounted the story, saying, ". . . and I felt so bad for them! They spent all that time putting it together, and it looked magnificent—I wish I'd taken a picture—and then they just had to turn around and tear it down. I felt awful."

---

46. The world of *Unedited* is . . . different from ours. I suppose the world in this book is, too.

But although Mike's mother clucked her tongue and joined in on the pity, clutching her offspring close to her in a comforting embrace that Mike secretly felt he was too old for but just as secretly enjoyed, Mike himself felt no disappointment at the day's events. Truthfully, some tiny inkling had opened up deep within him, some whisper of fresh air blowing into a hitherto-sealed cavern of his imagination: he had cared more for the building of the fort, it turned out, than for the playing in it. While George and the others had grumbled as they disassembled the structure, Mike had paid careful attention to the labor, to the way in which what had taken so long to build came down so quickly and so easily. He noted the way the boys stacked the blocks against the wall, and while he said nothing to push them in one direction or another, he realized that by placing *his* blocks in specific spots at specific times, he could force the other boys to place their blocks in a certain pattern, replicating precisely the original configuration of the blocks, pre-fort.

Building things and thinking of building things and tearing them down . . . It was the day Mike became an architect, though he did not know that word, could not spell it, would have mispronounced it as "archie-teckt" had it been shown to him.

"Yes," Mike whispered. "That's it. That's my first memory." He wiped a tear from his eye. "I had forgotten. Forgot how deep it went. I always told people I loved the aesthetics or the art or the science or the precision, but it goes back—"

"Uh-huh, yeah, I know." I stopped him before he could get too lachrymose. There was no point. "Wait. This next bit is going to be very dialogue-intensive. I'm going to switch over to a transcript style. I like that style, and it's worked for me in the past. I'm getting tired of coming up with little things for us to do and little reactions for us to have during this conversation. It's one of the problems I've always had with dialogue. Trying to figure out how many times to say 'he said,' how many times to have someone arch an eyebrow. How boring is it to show reactions? How boring is it *not* to show reactions? So let's just switch over for a little while."

LYGA: There. That'll work. As I was saying, it's not a bad little scene. Or moment. There aren't Saturday-morning cartoons anymore in my world, but in your world I think there are. So there are. But the whole memory is sort of based on something that happened to me as a kid,[47] but I gave it some extra emotional oomph because of your architecture thing.

GRAYSON: Architecture "thing"!

LYGA: But do kids even get naptime in kindergarten anymore? I thought I read somewhere that they don't. Maybe my copyeditor will know.[48] I don't care one way or the other. Even if they don't, I'll probably still leave it in. The fact of the matter is, every story has some sort of anachronism crawling through it, regardless of how assiduously you scan the details. I like the naptime bit, and it's not going to ruin the story for anyone.

GRAYSON: Architecture "thing"?

LYGA: I'll probably leave it in anyway . . . What are you complaining about now?

[*Grayson pounds the ground with a fist and looks up at Lyga with blazing eyes.*]

---

47. The fort was actually a boat, and there was no war-play involved. And, obviously, it did not instill in me a desire to become an architect.
48. COPYEDITOR'S NOTE: I have no idea, sorry!

GRAYSON: It isn't just some architecture "thing"! It's my life! It's the most important thing in my life other than Phil, and the way things are going these days, I guess it'll probably be the only thing that matters to me, when it's all said and done. So don't minimize it like that.

LYGA: Oh, please. Mike, you care about architecture, but it doesn't matter. None of it's authentic. I did a bunch of research for you, but that's all. I don't know anything about architecture, so you don't, either. You just know the stuff I've made up and picked up here and there.

GRAYSON: I'm . . . I'm not really going to be an architect?

LYGA: You're not "really" anything. I can make you an architect, though. I can make you anything I want. All I have to do is write it and it's true. All I have to do is write it and then they read it and it's true. I mean, I could do this:

CHAPTER 23

Mike looked out at the audience, trying to find his parents and his brother among the hundreds gathered on College Y's New Quad. He didn't want to take long, but he was one of only a bare hundred graduating today from College Y's School of Architecture, so his momentary hesitation would hardly be noticed. He spotted them roughly midway between the stage and the archway leading out of New Quad and selfishly stole a moment of everyone's time to wave to them.

He'd done it. As of today, he was an architect. The diploma in his hand proved it.

"But what would that accomplish?" I asked, dropping out of transcript mode. "Come on. Walk with me."

He finally took my hand, and I helped him to his feet. Together, we walked around to the front of the house, where the long driveway made its unerring, straight-line way to the road. "Still feels weird to see the driveway paved," I told him. "It was a loose stone driveway the whole time I lived here. Shoveling snow from it was a bitch in the winter."

"Why are you doing this to me?" he asked. "Why are you showing me all of this? All I want—"

"—is Phil. I know. Why am I showing you all of this, Mike? Because just once I would like someone to understand, that's why. Do you have any idea what it's like to be God? To be all-powerful and powerless at the same time? God can do anything for anyone, anywhere . . . except for himself.

"And that is the torture of being God. That is the dark secret of being God. God lives in hell, Mike. Why should you have it any better?"

Before he could respond, I turned around and pointed to the house. "This is where it all started. I have a memory of being about six or seven years old and wanting to be a writer, but it never really kicked in—I never started writing—until my parents got divorced and I had to move to Fuck-All, USA. But this is the house I lived in when I was in high school, which is when I came up with the idea for Inframan and for *Inframan*. Come on." I gestured for him to follow as I walked down the driveway. He waited a moment, then jogged to catch up.

"Where are we going?"

"The past," I told him. "With each step we take, the neighborhood around us regresses into history, becoming closer and closer to the way it was when I moved here."

"Oh." A beat. "That's actually sort of cool. I mean, think of how you could observe architecture—"

"Mike, stop it with the architecture shit, okay?" I said wearily. "I'm tired of typing that word."

"Sorry."

"Anyway," I went on as we crested a hill and met the intersection of the street and the main drag through town, "this is what it looked like when I moved here."

Ahead of us was the empty road, two lanes of naked blacktop cutting through farm country. By now, we'd walked far enough that the history regression bullshit that I invented[49] had returned the area to 1980 or so. Or at least, how I remembered it in 1980. A single gas station / convenience store waited across the street. Other than that, there were just empty fields and—in the distance—corn and soybeans.

"This is what it looked like when I moved here. And this is what I wanted to evoke in *The Astonishing Adventures of Fanboy and Goth Girl*,

---

49. Be honest, though—it would make a kick-ass special effect in a movie, right?

this sense of isolation and desolation, of utter hopelessness for anyone who dreams of anything more. But somehow the little shit-kicking town became bigger than I intended. And as quickly as the second book, there were all sorts of restaurants and even a mall with a movie theater. It still had a small-town feel to it—mainly because the characters kept bitching about how it was a small town—but for me it wasn't what I originally intended. What I intended was this, the way the town was originally. Just barren and empty and backward and . . . Fuck, there wasn't even a Pizza Hut here until my senior year of high school!"

I asked him,	"And this is where you came up with me?"	, he asked me.
He waggled a hand in the air in a "so-so" motion.	"Sort of. I came up with the other Mike Grayson, the one from *Inframan*. And when I went to college, I started to write *Inframan*. Got about a third of the way through it, too, and had the whole thing mapped out."	I waggled a hand in the air in a "so-so" motion.
I figured it couldn't hurt to pretend to be interested, so I asked,	"What happened?"	I can't decide if he's genuinely interested or just feigning interest to get on my good side. I created him, but I can't tell, and it's sort of bothersome. But I never give up an opportunity to talk about my writing.

He told me,	"The anxiety of influence happened. You know what that is?"	, I said.
I answered,	"Sort of."	He sounded convincing, but I didn't entirely believe him.
And because he can't just accept "sort of" as an answer, he had to go blathering on and explain it to me.	"It's when you freak out because you figure that what you're trying to accomplish has already been done by someone else."	Which is really boiling it down to the essence, but there you have it.
But I have to admit I was curious. A bit.	"Done better, you mean?"	he asked, and of course that would be his primary concern. I shrugged.

"Possibly. Maybe. Doesn't really matter. All that matters is that it's been done before, and that makes it less original, less innovative, less attractive. In my case, I had an idea for a book where the characters come to realize they're just characters in a book, and one of them even gets to meet the author. But then there was a comic book series called *Animal Man*—"

"Animal Man? Seriously?"

"Just listen. The writer—Grant Morrison—did something similar, where the character realized he was just in a comic book and gets to meet Morrison. And I freaked out, wondering exactly *when* I'd come up with my own take on that. Was it really before I read *Animal Man*? Or was it after, and I was just playing memory tricks on myself? How original was I? Worse: Would readers think I was ripping him off?

"And I have to tell you—it's not just the stuff that I *could* have ripped off. It's stuff that I couldn't *possibly* have ripped off. Like a scene in *Infra-man* where Angia is eating breakfast with her husband and they're totally not communicating well at all and she's watching him concentrate on eating his eggs. It's similar to a scene in *Madame Bovary* . . . but guess what? When I wrote that scene in *Inframan*, I hadn't read *Madame Bovary* yet! That wouldn't stop people of accusing me of ripping it off, though, so what the hell was I supposed to do about that?"

"I can see that," he said with sympathy. "So you stopped working on *Inframan*."

"Yeah. For years. But you know what? People have been doing this kind of shit forever, in all kinds of media. Bugs Bunny cartoons where he looks into the camera or redraws the action. David Addison talks to the audience in *Moonlighting*. Old Justice League comics where Cary Bates or Elliot Maggin meet the superheroes they write about. All of it. It's not the idea. It's the execution. It's all in *how* you do it. I did something similar to all of this in *Mangaman*, my first graphic novel."[50]

Mike stared at me in disbelief. "You . . . you did this to someone else? You put someone *else* through this?"

"Well . . . sort of. It was played for fun there."

"I could make it work," he grumbled. "It's just about planning and designing and—"

"Mike. Please. You're not a fucking architect. Everything you know about architecture came out of a copy of *Architecture for Dummies* I got from a used bookstore."

He shook his head vehemently. "No. No. This isn't right. This is all wrong. Why are you doing this to me? Why are you torturing me? Nothing's real? Nothing at all? What about the underwater hotel?"

"Well, I'm not sure about that one, to be honest with you. It might actually be sui generis, though I doubt it. I sort of came up with it on my own one night, joking around with someone. And then I forgot about it until she mentioned it again a month later and I realized that I needed to put it in the book. It just sort of fit."[51]

"That's how you create the universe? You don't have a master plan, you just come up with stuff and if it 'sort of fits' you use it?"

50. Published in fall 2011 by Houghton Mifflin Books for Children and available at bookstores and comic book stores everywhere!

51. And somewhere between then and now, someone actually built a fucking underwater home in Dubai. And it's *not* the same as Mike's idea, but I just can't get into all of that right now. Goddamn reality, messing up a good story . . .

He was angry—fuming, in fact—going red in the face in a way I never have. One more difference between him and me.

"Well . . . sure. That's how everything is created, really. I realized I was writing about myself, in a way. There were people—well, one person in particular—who was like, 'You shouldn't be writing this crazy book. It's too big and it's too ambitious. Who do you think you are to try something like that? What makes *you* so great?' Nice, huh? And, you know, that's the sort of comment I used to get when I was trying to break into comic books and into publishing—'Don't even try this, kid. It's too much for you.'"

"'You're not Diller and Scofidio. Or Frank Lloyd Wright,'" Mike quoted angrily.

"Right! Exactly! Goddamn!" I paced furiously. "I mean, how the fuck do *they* know? All your professor saw was a couple of sketches in your sketchbook. And when I was trying to break in, all those editors saw were a few pages of my writing. How the fuck do they know? You said that to your professor, remember?"

"'How do you know that? Maybe I am,'" he self-quoted.

"Yeah. I gave you that line because I once pitched a comic book idea to someone as 'Imagine Jack Kirby working on *Watchmen*.' And the response I got was 'Don't compare yourself to those guys. You aren't them.' And I wish . . . I wish I'd said what *you* said. That's why I gave it to you. I wish I'd said it, just once in my life."

"But it came from Phil," he told me. "You say you gave me the line, but it was only thinking of Phil that—"

"Ah, shit." Well, this is embarrassing. Fuck. Would any of you readers have even noticed? Anyway . . . "That's right. See, originally, you just said the line. But when I was revising, one of the problems with the book was that people were saying that Phil was a cipher. They couldn't figure out why you were so in love with her. So when I revised, I had her doing some cool shit—the plays, stuff like that—and also made her badass enough to inspire you to stand up for yourself."

"But—"

"Anyway, look, now I'm all pissed off because this little digression has fucked up the flow of the conversation. So I'm going to take it back to 'Yeah.'

"Yeah. I gave you that line because I wish I'd said it, just once in my life. Wish I'd had the courage just once. But I didn't, so I gave you the courage, Mike."

He stared at me. "Do I thank you for that?"

Thank me? "Why start now? Look, my point is this: the architecture stuff started out as just little details for the reader and then became more important to me. And especially that underwater hotel. Something miraculous happened there. Some truly amazing serendipity. Which is that I met this guy named Chris Cummings who actually designs aquariums—the big ones, not the ones for, like, tropical fish at home—for a living. So I sat down with him and asked him all sorts of questions, and suddenly 'your' idea became more important. So, thanks for that, Chris. I appreciate the time you spent with me talking about that stuff."

"Hey!" He waved a hand in front of my face. "Talk to *me*, not . . . not some *reader*."

He cast about, looking for said "reader," only to realize that we were in a new place. Small room. A massive Yale-issue desk with my old Macintosh Classic sitting atop it. Curtains that I never opened. Two doors—one led to the hallway and one led to an emergency exit that I never needed and never explored, lest I set off the alarm.

Mike gaped, twisting and turning to look around, as if the road we'd been on before would be right behind us instead of a closed door that led, when opened, to the stairwell landing directly across which lay the rest of my senior suite, perpendicular to which stood the door to the common bathroom.

"Where are we? What are we doing here?"

"Oh. Right. This is my senior dorm at Yale. I moved us here without mentioning it a few paragraphs ago. This is where I actually wrote about a hundred pages of *Inframan* and planned out my other books—*Redesigning You* and *His Darkness* and *American Sun* and all the others." I passed a hand over my face. "Jesus. I had this idea . . . I was going to take you on a tour of everywhere I lived, talking about the status of this book and of *Inframan* at each stop. Like how I decided George drank Stella Artois because when I was working on that part of the book, I lived near a bar with a big Stella

Artois sign out front and I walked past it every day. But that just sounds so boring now. I don't want to write it, you don't want to hear it, and I don't think readers want to read it. So, look, let's cut to the core, okay?"

"And the core is . . . ?" He teetered between giving a shit and wanting to rip my head off.

I shrugged, probably the one thing guaranteed to piss him off even more. "The core is that Inframan always wins, Mike. I never finished *Inframan*. I failed. I worked on it in college, suffered the anxiety of influence, and stopped. Tried to get back into it sporadically over the years, but never could. And then on August 5, 2005, that version of me died and the book went away. Or at least I thought it did.

"Because then something happened that spawned *this* book, the one you're in right now. A new Mike Grayson. The same author, but different. Different world, similar problems. Different book, but . . . somehow the same. A book that didn't shrink from the anxiety of influence, but reveled in it. Even there, though, he won. Because no one was willing to publish this thing. It took more than ten goddamn years. More failure. I thought . . . I thought I created him, Mike, but in a way, he created me. My failures made me who I am."

He wasn't paying attention anymore, though. Earlier phrases had caught his attention, his imagination.

"Why did you come back to the book?" he asked. "Why did you reconfigure it into . . ." He gestured around us. ". . . this? What happened? What made you return to it?"

I smiled at him. "I lost her, Mike."

"Who?" he asked, but he knew. He knew and yet he asked anyway.

"I lost Phil," I told him, in a nice, suitably dramatic moment to break a chapter.

But hell, we're getting close to the end and paper costs money, so let's push on without a chapter break, all right?

"Somehow, it seemed to come together. All of these disparate elements from my life. They joined together with the old ideas from *Inframan* to make you. You love Phil. You lose Phil. One letter separates those ideas, Mike. In your world, the difference between loving and losing is a typo. It's simple. In fiction, it's simple to break and simple to fix. It's so much more complicated in my world. You think you have it bad? Think of us poor saps in the Realm Above.

"Anyway, I had always liked the idea of writing a book that was out of order, a book that started partway in, then jumped around, where chapters would be out of order. And I started thinking about that, started thinking about someone who could do that from within a book, someone who could edit from the inside. Because that, I realized, was what I was trying to do with my own life: I was always looking back at emails she'd sent me, things she'd said to me, things I'd said to her . . . always thinking, *If I had done/said* this *instead of* that*, then maybe she would have reacted* this *way instead of* that *way*, and blah, blah, blah. It would be a perfect world. We would be together. I kept trying to read her tea leaves. Kept replaying conversations over and over in my head, poring over her emails and text messages, trying to find a logic to it all, trying to figure out when her character fell out of love with my character. But we weren't characters. And none of it made any sense. And, truthfully, that drove me a little bit crazy.

"So I decided to make it a story, a novel. It would be a big, ugly, complicated thing, like love, like romance, like life. But here's the thing: real life is messy. It doesn't make sense. The best we can do on the page is mimic that, but if you try to be too random, people get bored or get annoyed. So I needed some sort of force to show up and move things along, and that ended up being my old frenemy, Inframan.

"So Phil started out as one woman in particular. One experience. And something happened in the writing. Despite my notes and my outlines and my planning, she began to merge with other women. So even though she's meant to represent / stand in for one woman in my life, she's somehow become *all* the women in my life, even though she doesn't represent them." I clucked my tongue and leaned back in my chair. It had been twenty years since I'd leaned back in this chair, but it felt like twenty seconds had passed. "Is there a literary term for that? There should be. Maybe it's 'reverse synecdoche.'"[52]

---

52 If there is a term for it, you'd think I would know it. Or take the time to look it up. But at

Mike shook his head, not understanding.

"But here's the thing, Mike. Here's the funny thing: I originally came up with the idea for this book because I wanted her back. But then you know what happened? Do you?"

He shook his head again.

And I smiled. (Truthfully, it's the first honest, happy smile in this whole damn book.) "I met someone else. And that's the answer, Mike. That's the answer to your heartbreak and your heartache: You meet someone else. You don't redesign the universe to bring your lost love back. You give up. You give up on blue-haired Phil, you give up on the history-made sheets, and you move on with your life. That's how it works.

"At first, I thought writing this book would help me get through things. And then—before I even started the actual writing, when I was still in the plotting stage—I met someone new and amazing and wonderful, and suddenly that wasn't necessary anymore. But I wrote it anyway, because I thought that maybe it would help kids who are going through losing their first loves. You know? Sort of show them that no one is worth all that angst. Or at least that there's a way to get through to the other side. And now . . ."

"Now, what? What?"

"I don't know. I've come all this way. I have written and rewritten. I don't know anymore. I don't know what the point is."

"So you're saying this book you're writing, the whole story of my existence, my life—you're saying it's all pointless? That you're just going through the motions?"

"Maybe. What if I am? So what?"

He found the courage and the strength to stand up. "If you don't have a point anymore, then just let me have Phil back. End the book with the two of us together."

I shook my head. "Weren't you listening to me? That's not the point at all. You move on. You meet someone else."

"But I don't want to meet someone else. I want her."

"What is 'her,' though, Mike? Really. Do you want Phil as Phil, or

---

this point, I honestly can't be bothered.

does she just represent something for you? If you go back and look at the whole of your relationship, you see that it's all very centered on you. Phil has little to no agency, which is super-unfeminist of me, I admit. There were some early readers who got really, *really* upset by the treatment of Phil. Which is fine because everyone is entitled to their opinion, obviously, but it also misses the point of the book entirely. Phil had a very specific function in the story. You *all* have very specific functions, and you bump up against the limitations of those functions all the time. Phil has little to no agency, but the fact is *none* of you have agency, really. I'm controlling the whole goddamn thing. You all exist to make a point. And I'm a random straight white dude writing a book that is deliberately solipsistic and stridently unempathetic. Not because I think straight white dudes are awesome, but just because . . . if you're writing a book designed to show people what it's like inside your brain when you write, you have to limit yourself to what's inside your brain. The only character in the book who is fully realized and actually matters is *me*.[53]

"Everyone else was a tough balancing act—like, you needed to be selfish, but at the same time, I had to make Phil cool enough that readers wouldn't reject your devotion to her. But Phil isn't really a person. She's a secondary character in the novel, man. She has blue hair because I wanted her to stand out. You objectify the living hell out of her because that's all you're capable of doing. It's all I gave you. And I probably objectified *my* Phil, if I'm being honest. So it's no wonder that relationship fell apart for me, and it's no wonder your relationship fell apart: Her belief in you isn't enough. Her faith isn't enough. What did you guys have in common, anyway, besides, as one early reader put it, 'Lots of great fucking?'"

"It was more than that," he muttered.

"Was it? And, hey—about all of that fucking . . . Did you ever stop to wonder what was going on there? Like, maybe it wasn't all that great for her?"

"No. She said . . ." He stopped. Thought. Remembered.

"Right. She never said anything. You want her so badly that you . . .

---

53. I sort of can't believe I have to say this. It seems so obvious to me. But then again, I'm me and you're not.

Look, did you ever think of maybe just trying to be cool to her? Or just talking to her? No, you just went ahead and tried to realign the fundamental nature of the universe in order to get her back."

He nodded slowly, resigned. "Okay, so what do I do?"

"Nothing. I'll do all the work. We're going to have a flashback to earlier in the book. I hate flashbacks, by the way. They're not real. They don't exist in real life. Convenient, huh?"

"Can we go now?" he asked.

"Go? We're there. Here. Whichever."

EDITED

"I always thought it would be cool if flashbacks worked like this. Instead of just summarizing the moment, actually relive it. I guess that's similar to film, in some respects, but why not? It's sort of cool, I think."

"You're really impressed with yourself, aren't you?"

"Someone has to be. So, check it out: Here's the moment where things could have changed. Right here."

"She wanted me to read to her . . ."

"Yeah. She was ready. She was receptive. You could have read to her and then told her you loved her and it would have all worked out. And for your own reasons— creeped out by the paternity of it, comparing yourself to *him*—you couldn't do it. You wouldn't do it. So you lost her. Right there. Right here."

(also true), although I haven't decide[d] if I'll get in.

[bi]gger truth is that we're in Phil's bed an[d] [talkin]g.

mom—perennially single, never married [...attac]hed—considers herself a "cool mom." She does not [...] her daughter and I have "safe sex" in[...] [Phi]l's fifteenth birthday, stocked their share[d...] [vari]ety pack of condoms. Still, Phil and I ag[ree...] [to] hear your O noises, it's just way too cre[epy...] [th]us we abstain unless the house is empty. [...] [...hear Phil's] mother's car in the driveway in the silen[ce] between us, we pull apart.

"Read to me," she says.

"What?"

"Read to me." Phil curls up and points to a wa[ll] shelf I have noticed several times, crammed with *Wind in the Willows*, A. A. Milne, Beatrix Potter, other venerable friends left behind in the old precin[ct of childhood] hood when we packed our innocence onto a truck a[nd moved to] the new town of Growing Up. A sudden terror sei[zed me...] dated *him* almost from day one, holding hands wi[th...]

Mike's voice was nothing more than a whisper. Well, words on a page *and* a whisper: "You mean, I could have done it? I could have actually fixed everything?"

"Well, maybe. I thought long and hard about that. I decided that it was a cheat not to have there be a way to do it. And I was rooting for you, man, I really was. But you just couldn't do it."

"You weren't rooting for me. You knew how it would end all along."

"Well, yeah, that's true, too. But let me tell you something, Mike: There's a problem with this scenario. Even with what I've just shown you."

"What's that?"

"You didn't love her. Not then. Not yet. You didn't love her until she was gone. And that's tragic and sad and stupid. But the only time you could have won her over was a time when you didn't really, truly, *need* to win her over. And then there's the other problem with this solution. And as one friend who read an early draft put it: 'And, frankly, at the end when Barry Lyga points out the moment that could have changed things . . . well, although I liked the fact that BL put in a solution, the truth is, I just don't believe that anything could have changed things—the timing just wasn't right for them.' And maybe she was right. She also pointed out that your ability to control her could be seen as misogynistic. It may be. But you're able to control *everyone*, regardless of gender or sex, including Phil's old/new boyfriend. So if it is misogynistic, it's not *only* misogynistic. But, hey—you say 'potato,' I say 'spud.' Maybe it would have worked, maybe it wouldn't have. Beats me."

He stomped his foot, as close to a temper tantrum as his self-respect would allow. "Is this all just laughs to you? You keep saying it's my responsibility, but you created all of it. You made me, you made her, you made me lose her—"

"Look at it this way," I said to him. "Take comfort in this: It's not like you ever really loved her. You just think you did. You're nineteen. You don't know what real love is yet."

He bristled and actually—I give him credit for this—took a step toward me, an act of aggression in the face of unrelenting power that

I didn't expect until I wrote it. "I do so love her! I love her more than myself. More than the universe."

"Yeah, that's not love, Mike. That's obsession. There's a difference. You're too young. Kids don't know what love is."

He flung his hands in the air. "We can know what love is. It's adults who have forgotten, so they cling to their poor substitute and yell at kids who dare to live with real love. Pure love. Love without compromise or distraction. Hell, when you're a kid you've got all the energy and all the free time in the world. You'll never have the chance to devote more to love ever again in your life."

I sighed. "Nice. Nice speech."

"Thanks."

"Yeah, that's not even your dialogue. I lifted it from my second book.[54]"

"Oh, come on! That's not fair!"

He said nothing after that, and we stood in silence for a few moments, each of us thinking. I knew what he was thinking, of course, but dialogue will do a better job explaining it:

"Could you . . ." he said after a moment's hesitation, "could you make me a *different* way? Change me so that I don't want her anymore?"

It was a decent enough idea, and sure, I had the power to do it. But . . .

"No. That would . . . Look, that would go against the reader's expectations, okay? The reader is invested in your story because you're a kid who loves a girl so much that you broke through the ends of the universe and challenged God for her. I can't just have you change your mind at this point. The whole story would fall apart."

"It's not a story! It's my life."

"They're the same thing."

"Fine, then it's my life story, but—"

"Life story?" I laughed at the absurdity of it, but also because I was

54. *Boy Toy*, published in 2007 by Houghton Mifflin Books for Children. The quotation in question comes on page 386.

finally using a line I'd written early in the planning days of the novel: "There's no such thing as a life story. Life isn't a story. Stories can be fixed and modified and changed and revised. Life is unedited."

Big tears rolled down his face, and his shoulders—his entire being— slumped in the most abject defeat I've ever seen. "I've had enough, okay? I've had enough." He dropped to his knees and clasped his hands before him, his face tilted to look up at me in the familiar penitent's pose. "I am down on my knees, begging you, praying to you: Please. Give me back Phil. Please, Almighty God. Please."

"Flattery doesn't do it, Mike. I can't give Phil back to you. It's just not that easy. Things have gotten too complicated."

"You met someone new," he pointed out, scrambling and desperate. "You got a happy ending. Why can't I have one, too?"

"Who says it was happy? We're not even together anymore. It was absolutely insane—the craziest breakup in my life. Holy shit." I shivered. "I don't even like thinking about it."

"Jesus!" he exclaimed, throwing his hands in the air in complete defeat. "God! Does it ever work out for *anyone*?"

"Stop being so melodramatic. Love's not going anywhere. Though, you know, it feels like it when the person you love doesn't love you anymore. Anyway, my kind of happy ending wouldn't work for you. I was able to move on from Phil. You can't. You're incapable. I'm not sure how I could give you a happy ending, if you want to know the truth. Not without wrecking the whole construct of the story. I mean, sometimes it takes years and years to get over someone, to learn the lessons of that relationship, to move on. It took me ten years to land a publisher for this thing. It should probably take just as long for you to process your loss, figure out what you did wrong, grow as a person . . . Do you have, like, ten years to spare?"

"Ten years! I can't wait ten years to forget her. To get over her. Does it really take that long? God!" He twisted in on himself, clutching at his gut as though nauseated. "Ten more years like this? I can't handle that. How am I supposed to live with that?"

"One day at a time. Just like the rest of us."

He shook his head miserably.

"Right," I said. "If I've done my job, at this point everyone wants you to end up with Phil. But you shouldn't, Mike. You really shouldn't. It would be a cop-out. But right now, everyone wants that. They want me to find a way around the ending that Inframan revealed."

"The one where I'm in a room, alone." Still on his knees, but now slumped, staring at my feet.

"Yeah. That one. Endings are tricky motherfuckers. People are rarely happy with my endings, for example. People like everything tied up in a neat package; people like the kiss. They like the ride into the sunset. But I don't seem to be able to give them that. I don't know why. It's not that I have something *against* that sort of ending. I just can't make them work for me in my own books. They feel like cop-outs somehow. Here's something Scott Westerfeld said after reading one of my novels:

"So, you see? Endings are problematic for me. People always complain about my endings. I never do a good job with them. I'm always happy with them, but other people aren't. It comes down to this: I don't know *how* to give you a happy ending, kid. Fuck, I couldn't give myself one." I brightened and snapped my fingers as though I'd just realized something, though the next sentence was written more than a year before the current one. "That's the problem: We can't ask other people to fix our lives; we have to fix them ourselves. Which, I've just realized, is the through line for the whole book. You have to fix these things for yourself. You tried." I sighed. "And I've been writing this book for a long, long time. It started . . . God, the actual writing started almost exactly a year ago, the planning six months before that. But the idea of it . . ."[55]

I shook my head. Something had just occurred to me. An overt brainstorm, or more accurately a brain thunderstrike, a bolt hurled by my personal Zeus—Inframan—from the cloudy depths of my subconscious mind. A memory. More accurately, a cluster of them from childhood.

"I always tried to put myself in my stories. Going back long, long before I ever read King's *Dark Tower* or Morrison's *Animal Man*. I remember being in maybe fourth grade and starting a science fiction novel, which was going to be about some kind of futuristic rivalry between my direct descendant and a direct descendant of Thomas Edison. It was probably the comic books. The fucking comic books. The ones where the characters cross universes and meet other versions of themselves. I was miserable as a kid, Mike. I guess that idea appealed to me, the idea that I was a wreck, but that there was another version of me out there that was happy. And that was just one step away from wanting to *be* that version. I never wanted to be real, Mike. I wanted to be *fiction*. I wanted to be make-believe because in make-believe . . ."

I trailed off.

No point.

"So what do you think, Mike? You met God. You did it. Was she worth it? Was Phil worth it?"

He didn't hesitate: "Yes."

"I'm shocked," I said sarcastically.

"She's smart and talented and opinionated and supportive," he said heatedly. "Of *course* she's worth it."

"All qualities you wish you possessed. She reflects what you want to be. Do you think that's a good basis for love?"

He said nothing, thinking.

"And what about your traveling companions? Was it worth it to them? For them?"

---

55. Well, at the point of this draft, the actual writing began—oh, Jesus—MORE THAN TEN YEARS AGO. I'm getting old.

He tilted his chin in the air. "George believes in me. He came, too."

"Duh. George is gay, Mike.[56] He's in love with you.[57] Of course he came with you. You know how you'd go to the ends of the earth for Phil? Well, George would do the same for you. And has, in fact. You want to know what true love looks like? Try looking at George sometime and seeing more than just your sidekick or even your best friend. You went to the ends of the earth and climbed the Tower of Babel for Phil, who right now is safely at home, tangled up in her bedsheets with *him*, none the wiser that you've risked your life and very existence to try to win her back. George went to the ends of the earth and climbed the Tower of Babel for you, Mike. He risked his life and very existence alongside you, and he did it for the most selfless of reasons: love. Unrequited love, to be exact. He knew that if he helped you succeed, you would be with Phil again, but he did it anyway because more than anything else in the universe, George wants you to be happy. That's all he wants for you. And what do you want for him?"

Mike had realized this on some level, of course. And now he felt a whole universe of emotions too complicated to make for good conversation. "But I'm not gay," he said.

"No one said you have to be. Just appreciate what he's done. And why. Think about how miserable you are and put yourself in George's shoes."

"I never felt . . . You know, I never felt like I was as good a friend as I could have—"

I flapped my hands impatiently. "Yeah, yeah, I know—loaded down with all kinds of guilt. 'He's my best friend, but I'm not his.' Blah, blah, blah. I know. This book isn't about the nature of friendship. I just wanted to give you something to think about, is all. Something that isn't and wasn't you, and you and Phil. So you sit here"—I pulled over the chair—"and think about that. Meanwhile, I'm going to talk to Phil."

---

56. Second secret.
57. Third secret. (George would never tell it, but I will.)

He looked up at me hopefully from the chair, his expression depressingly puppylike.

"Not your Phil," I told him. "*My* Phil."

Okay, everyone. This next part isn't for you. Unless you're Phil. So I guess this is like one of those Choose Your Own Adventure books. If you are Phil, turn to page page 235. If you're not Phil, turn to page page 241.

Ready?

Go.

HELLO, PHIL

You know, I thought that when it came time to write this part of the book that I would have so much to say. But here I am, at this point having written more than two hundred thousand words in the unedited version of this book, then more words to patch the holes in this edited version. And it's not that I'm losing steam (there are days where I think I could spend the rest of my life working on just this book, could drop dead at a holographic keyboard some indeterminate time in the future with the ending still—always—a page away), but more that I've realized I have so little to say.

But, yeah—I couldn't admit it to Mike, though I will admit it here: when I started cobbling together this book, taking notes and outlining, my primary thought was that maybe it would help me win you back. I would open my soul to you, and you would be persuaded, convinced, and you would come running.

God, that seems so stupid now. Worse, it's a totally juvenile form of magical thinking, and you'd think that I'd be smart enough to avoid that. And yet, here we are.

Why?

That's a question I've been asking myself a lot lately. Is my life perfect? Of course not. No one's is. But things are pretty damn good, if you want to know the truth. I told Mike that I couldn't give myself a happy ending, but I got one anyway. Somehow. I'm engaged now. Married by the time this sees print.[58] So why on earth am I still writing this fucking book? Why on earth am I opening up these old wounds and pouring all manner of literary salt into them?

There's the selfish reason: I have to. The story is inside me, and this one in particular has been dying to get out since I was a kid, though I never in a million years thought it would take this particular form.

And there's the altruistic reason: maybe it will help someone.

I don't think those reasons conflict. There doesn't have to be any sort of mutual exclusion between selfishness and altruism. Maybe that's a lesson Mike needs to learn. I think it's possible to have both motivations at the same time. It's possible to be selfless and selfish in the same instant. I suspect, in fact, that this may be the secret of God: That He created the universe not for us, but for Himself. That He made us because He couldn't bear not to, not out of love. But that doesn't mean that He can't also love us.

In any event, if I believed in God, that's the kind of God I would believe in.

Wow. How the hell did I get from you, Phil, to some sort of half-assed theology?

It's all tangled up in my mind and in my heart. You've transmuted into every woman I ever spent time with, every ex of every stripe. A part of me thinks I should use this space to apologize, to tell you—all of you in general, but you specifically, of course—that I'm sorry for any pain I may have caused you, for any hurt I let linger. And then there's the part of me (I suspect it sounds like a dragon and smells of chocolate syrup) that laughs at that idea, that says, "Wow, Lyga—what a fucking egomaniac you are! Do you really think any of them need or want your contrition? Do you think you're so important that any hurt you inflicted lingers after all this time to any of them?"

And since that comes from me, it seems I've pulled off the neat

---

58. Not just married—we have two kids now, the lights of my life. That's how fucking long it's taken to publish this thing!

trick of writing a book that manages to encapsulate utter self-loathing and unrelenting narcissism at the same time. That's fitting, I suppose.

Thanks for the ego check, Inframan. I appreciate it. I probably needed it.

So, Phil. Here we are. You and me, connected by the strange combination of time travel and telepathy that is writing. Along with any number of recalcitrant readers who decided to ignore their instructions and read this anyway.

Phil, I loved you. All of the "yous" that there are and were. I was never able to say it or to prove it, I guess. I'm trying to be better. A better man. Person.

That's the lesson. The lesson Mike can't learn, because I won't let him learn it. The lesson I want my readers to learn through his example, his cautionary tale.

Love is not fungible, but love is also not irreplaceable. That cute guy in gym class? The guy who first said "I love you"? The girl who first said you were her world?

Yes, they are special. And dear. First loves are special and unique. But here's a secret:

All loves are special and unique.

Surrender is not failure when it serves to promote success. You let go of one swinging vine not because you can't hold it any longer but, rather, to leap to the next one. And the next. And the next. Progress. The future.

That moment between vines? Where gravity says, *Oh yes—I remember you!* and threatens to drag you down out of the sky? Oh, I know. I know. That moment is terrifying and horrifying and so awful that you'd rather just cling to that first vine forever.

But you can't. You shouldn't. You mustn't.

The funny thing, of course, is that Inframan has won once again. That little fucker always wins, even though he's the God of Failure. Because I've failed at what I set out to do.

I wanted to write something Truly Great. Something that was undeniably Art. Regardless of Zusak and Moore and Morrison and Bates and Maggin and Barth and Fox and King and all of them. I had to just plow ahead and tell my story the way I wanted to tell it. Fuck the anxiety of influence.

But I failed. I failed because it ended up being just another stupid love story.

Anyway, Phil, thanks for reading this long. If you even bothered. I wish I had some sort of grand answer for you here. I wish I could explain me or you or the book or anything. But I don't have any answers.

All I have is an ending.

Time to get there, I think.

Yes. Yes, it's time.

So, here we are, you and I. We're at the end.

Almost.

The problem here is that my editor, the redoubtable, infinitely patient *** *********, had a really great suggestion.

(Yes, it's possible for editors to have really great suggestions, despite what you may have read to this point.)

He thought that there should be a chapter from Phil's point of view. And I have to tell you, I fucking *loved* that idea. Some of his other ideas? Not so psyched about them, honestly. But that one! That one was pure gold.

We agreed that Phil should speak at the end of the book. And the problem we've run into is this: In the big book (in *Unedited*), after I say "Yes. Yes, it's time," there's still some stuff that happens before we get to the epilogue, so there's plenty of room for Phil to speak.

(Of course there's an epilogue in a pretentious fucking book like this.)

But in *this* book, *** went ahead and cut everything after "Yes. Yes, it's time," and jumped right to the epilogue. Where's the space for Phil? Doesn't it seem weird to say "It's time" and then suddenly there's this Phil chapter out of nowhere?

*** rethought his idea. Maybe, he suggested, we don't need the Phil chapter.

But it was too late. I was in love with the idea and I'd already written half of it. So we decided just to tell you, the reader: It's coming. It's coming on the next page, in fact. And then the epilogue and then, with our thanks for your forbearance and your time, we'll be done.

CHAPTER 24[59]

Phil sat on her bed, a copy of A. A. Milne's *The House at Pooh Corner* unopened on her lap. She had a memory of reading the book and a memory of being read the book, but right now she was most concerned with this thought: Did the book actually exist?

She'd never experienced such an existential crisis before. Or perhaps existential crisis was too kind a way to describe it. Perhaps psychotic break from reality was more truthful.

The book weighed on the tops of her thighs. It had heft; gravity dragged it down. When she ran the pad of her right index finger along its edge, the smooth board of the cover indented her flesh ever so slightly. She knew that if she did the same with a page, she would incur a paper cut.

This is a different world, she thought. Did A. A. Milne exist in this

---

59. EDITOR'S NOTE: At first I argued for the inclusion of this chapter. Given that Mike (by his own admission) objectifies Phil, I wanted her to have a voice. Then I argued against it; I wasn't sure if Barry could give her the voice she deserves. That's where I left it: No Phil. But Barry wrote the chapter anyway. Authors are obstinate like that. They are egomaniacal [expletive deleted]. The truth? I would rather spend time in prison than hang out with most authors. On the other hand, editing is as subjective as any other form of engaged criticism, and even though I would never say this to Barry or any writer of his caliber, I can (very infrequently) be wrong . . . as far as the best story is concerned. I also believe 100 percent that honest writers—those who read obsessively and do the work and put the time in—should have unfettered freedom to experiment. So in this unique instance I leave it to you, the reader, to judge Barry's writing.

world? Is that name an anagram for some other author? Pooh, we can be certain, is fiction, but is Milne fiction, as well?

She knew that books written for children and teens and such were called nonadult books, to distinguish them from books written for, well, adults. And yet for some reason, she thought of this as a children's book, not a nonadult book. And the copy of *The Unlikely Tale of Geekster and the Vampiress* that had appeared on her bookshelf . . . It, too, was nonadult, and yet she couldn't help thinking of it as young adult.

According to quantum physics—about which Phil knew absolutely nothing except for what is to follow—the universe is not unique and solitary. There is/was a multitude of universes, each one with its own worlds and lives and loves. A staple of spec-fic (which, for some reason, her brain nagged her to think of as sci-fi), such universes existed in parallel to her own.

What if, she wondered, books themselves were portals to those other universes? Or at least representations of those universes? That would mean that every book—no matter its fidelity to reality—took place in a world that was not reality. And furthermore, that every book—no matter how unreal—was, in fact, fact, not fiction.

The implications would have spun her, if not for the weight of the book in her lap.

She thought that perhaps her own world was not all it seemed, as though there could be more to it. And so she turned. And she looked at you. And she said this:

I'm Phil.

(Before you ask: Yes, the blue hair is natural. No, I won't explain.)

More accurately, I'm an approximation of Phil, a version made of ink on paper as opposed to blood, bone, and flesh. And I'm also an approximation of the Phil who exists as a synecdoche—or perhaps more accurately, a metonymy—of the women he knew and chose to replicate, in cyborg-like pieces, on the page.

And so here and now, he is trying to write me as closely as a man can get to writing a woman. In fairness, he has an advantage—he created me, so technically no matter what he writes about me or for me, he can't be wrong. You can say, "Come on, Lyga, no woman would say that!" and he can simply sit back with a serene/smug expression and reply, "Phil would." And you can't say he's wrong. Or rather, you can, but then you would be wrong. Creator's advantage.

But he's trying. He's trying very hard not to play the God card. Not here. Not now.

Because we're at the end. The end is where truths are revealed. No one solves a mystery in the middle of the book. The killer is never unmasked halfway through the movie.

You haven't heard from me yet. Maybe you think I'm paper thin, a caricature more than a character. A weak female side character, developed purely as a prize for the male lead to pursue. An example of the male gaze in action and not much else.

Guess what? Yeah, I'm all of those things. And more. Some of it good, some of it bad.

Why? Because that's what fits the needs of the story. Because the story is about Mike and Phil, yes, but it is told via the mechanism of the quest for God, the pursuit of capital-*L* Love. Which is inherently unrealistic, and so you can't really expect all of the characters to be fully realized.

Even me, the most important female character in the book. As too often happens with female characters in male-driven stories, I become invisible and intangible to fit the needs of the story. No, it's not fair.

(This is where I'm supposed to say "Smash the patriarchy!" But this isn't that kind of book.)

You may be wondering, Do I love Mike? Do I not love Mike? Did I ever?

It almost doesn't matter at this point. Yeah, I know this is a love story, but so what? Love stories sometimes end in pain, in heartache. Sometimes they end inconclusively. Sometimes, like poor George's love story, they end unrequited.

Sometimes they end in a room, alone.

If you've read the book, you may wonder—love or not—exactly what I wanted from Mike. I felt as though my purpose in the book was to call Mike on his shit. And the problem, then, is that since he didn't like being called on his shit, he kept trying to edit the story to avoid those painful moments with me. Which ended in him editing our relationship out of existence entirely. Which, further, meant that I wasn't around to tell him how to fix it.

There's a moral in there, but you got this far—you'll figure it out.

What did I want from Mike? In the best of worlds, in the steadiest of timelines and iterations, I wanted him above all to be true to himself. To find that balance between selfishness and sacrifice. Because the world demands both from us. The only way to achieve and to proceed is by giving and hoarding. The trick is knowing when to do which.

Women know that better than men—we're the ones who get pregnant, after all, and you can't find a more potent metaphor for both sacrifice and greed than pregnancy. You have to think of only yourself, but of course you're also thinking of what's inside you. And then you have the baby, and you have to let it grow up and become its own person, but it still feels like a part of you. You have to sacrifice your own life and happiness for that kid, while all along trying to steal moments for yourself.

Pregnancy is where it all starts. Everything else rolls out from there. All life, all politics, all art proceed from that. For good and for ill.

Look, I would love to live in a world where reproduction was considered so awe-inspiring that women were accorded respect and power and equality because everyone recognized that the whole damn shooting match begins right there in the womb, the one thing we haven't figured out how to replace with plastic and glass and stainless steel. Yet.

But instead we live in a world where reproduction—and the shit that gets you to reproduction in the first place—generates hate, fear, contempt, misogyny, and lots and lots of fundraising for politicians.

At least, that's *my* world. I don't know what things are like in the pages of *your* book.

And speaking of the book—this doesn't even have anything to do with the book anymore. I'm just saying it because it's what I believe. And I bet someday Mike would believe it, too—he'd get there.

If he would let himself.

If he could get out of his own way.

Can he? Will he?

Well, like you, I don't know. What happens to characters after you close the book, anyway?

(Oh, and BTW: Smash the patriarchy. Smash that fucker to pieces, burn the pieces to ash, and piss on the ashes.)

Phil stopped speaking. She lifted the Milne book from her lap and decided whether or not to read it.

EPILOGUE

Ten years passed then, ten years whipping by in less time than it took to say it or to write it or to read it. Ten years passed in the time it takes to turn a page.

Many things happened to Michael Grayson in those ten years, but looking back on them, they were blurry and indistinct, none of them standing out. They were just "many things" that had happened to him in ten years.

He lived in the city still, had lived there since graduating with his degree in architecture. He had managed to make that happen despite a reputation in high school as a delinquent and a problematic student. That history no longer mattered. What mattered was that something had happened to him a decade ago, something that had compelled him to action, had compelled him to put his life together and rekindle the dream of architecture.

Now he worked for a firm that let him telecommute, so he spent many days just as he spent this one: alone, in a room. Crooked over his drawing table or leaning toward his computer screen, doing that which he loved: building.

His current project was a shopping center, surely the most journeyman of architectural tasks, but this one in particular struck a personal and resonant note. It was the first new shopping center to be built in the desert surrounding the city, abutting a hotel by an oasis.

On his computer, there were files in a folder marked "Dreams," files for a building made of elevators and a sprawling suite of hotel rooms underwater, this last inspired by a vague memory from long ago. He sometimes awoke at night, imagining he'd been there, that he'd sunk beneath the surface of the water in an elevator, friends at his side. Impossibly, there'd been rain.

But, no. That surely could not be. Could not have been.

His boss thought he was insane, but tolerably so. Mike didn't mind that reputation. There was something to be said for an insane artist, he thought. Artists should always try to achieve the impossible, to construct the unconstructable. In short, to do the things no one else thinks they should even bother doing.

Time for a break. He stood up from his drawing table and stretched, cracking his back satisfactorily and soothingly. As he did so, he glimpsed a set of keys on the very farthest corner of the table. They were not his keys; they had been forgotten. Again.

At just that moment, the doorbell rang.

Mike grinned. He went to the door, thinking of nothing but the door. The doorbell rang again before he got there.

"Just a sec!" he called.

He opened the door. He said,

HELLO, PHIL

¡CLOUD HACK SUCCESSFUL!

**Downloading contents of iMessage chat between
AUTHOR (Barry Lyga) and EDITOR**

LYGA: Hey, look, now that's all over, I just wanted to say . . .

LYGA: I was really skeptical when you first proposed this crazy idea of making a second, expurgated version of *Unedited* . . .

LYGA: And the process was sort of chaotic and I wasn't 100% sure of it until I was really deep into it . . .

LYGA: But I enjoyed it, in the end. I think it made a long, weird book even longer and weirder. Which is a good thing, in this case.

LYGA: So, thanks for pushing me.

*********: You're welcome!

LYGA: But I have to admit—I still prefer the big book.

*********: And it's still out there, for those who want to read it. I have to take this call.

LYGA: So . . . what do you think about a sequel?

[chat log indicates no response from *********]

ABOUT THE AUTHOR

Barry Lyga was the author of *Inframan, or The Coming of the Unpotent God*, as well as *American Sun, Redesigning You, For Love of the Madman*, and other novels. He died in 2005 with his last novel unfinished.

ABOUT THE AUTHOR

Barry Lyga is the author of *The Astonishing Adventures of Fanboy and Goth Girl*, *Boy Toy*, *Goth Girl Rising*, and the I Hunt Killers series, among others. He lives in New York City. Or Baltimore. Or New Jersey. Or, possibly, Edinburgh. Or somewhere he hasn't imagined yet. It all depends on when you're reading this book. In fact, he might not live in any of those places, or he could even be dead by now.